THE FEEIN' MARKET

At the Forfar Feein' Market beautiful and intelligent Rowena MacFarlane is hired by Angus Campbell to help his wife, Lizzie, with her small sons. But Rowena affects more than the running of the household.

Four men love her in their different ways and she loves them in return. Angus, her employer, wild Marek, the Irish gypsy who grew up with her, Tam Laird, the horseman, and Matthew Grey, the gambler, who lives his life on the throw of a dice. Only one is the father of Rowena's daughter. Only one has Rowena's heart.

THE FEEIN' MARKET

THE FEEIN' MARKET

by

Eileen Ramsay

Magna Large Print Books
Long Preston, North Yorkshire,
BD23 4ND, England.

British Library Cataloguing in Publication Data.

Ramsay, Eileen
    The Feein' Market.

    A catalogue record of this book is
    available from the British Library

    ISBN   0-7505-1759-X

First published in Great Britain in 1999
by D. C. Thomson & Co. Ltd.

Copyright © 1999 Eileen Ramsay

Cover illustration © Len Thurston by arrangement with
P.W.A. International Ltd.

The moral right of the author has been asserted

Published in Large Print 2002 by arrangement with
Mrs Eileen Ramsay

Magna Large Print is an imprint of Library Magna Books Ltd.

Printed and bound in Great Britain by
T.J. (International) Ltd., Cornwall, PL28 8RW

Springhill Farm,
May 1895

*She was so dark, so beautiful, so desirable...
This was insanity, madness, call it what you
will...*

*He loved his wife, had loved her from the first
moment he'd gone to work on her father's land.
But tonight the blood was rushing through his
veins, like a burn in spate, helped along by the
unaccustomed ale he had drunk.*

*He had no more control over the wildness that
raged within him than he had over the un-
trammelled winds that blew across the open
fields of Forfarshire every year, carrying seed
and soil with them.*

He swore now, but at himself, at his weakness.

*'Go home, Angus – don't give in to her
charms ... no matter how desperately you want
her. Be sensible, man.'*

*But when the door of the bothy opened and
light and the beautiful girl spilled out together,
he stood up and waited for her, and knew full
well what would happen.*

*Tomorrow he would suffer and tomorrow and
tomorrow, but the sin would be his and the
suffering, his and his alone.*

She was beside him now, so close that he could

smell her sweetness.

He whispered her name, pulling her wordlessly into the great barn... His lips sought her hungrily and all thoughts of tomorrow vanished as he yielded to his desires...

The roads to Forfar had been full well before daybreak. Carts were piled high with goods to sell, to barter, or to exchange...

Bakers with oven-fresh loaves; innkeepers with barrels of ale, sure to be empty before nightfall; the sweetie wife with her home-made confections; gingerbread sellers, chestnut vendors, and men and boys on bicycles, or simply treading out...

All were heading into the valley for the Whitsun Feein' Market – the hiring fair.

Since it was May, the roads were especially busy: all the farm workers changed contracts at Whit, except for those agreed in Dundee, of course, where they always had to be contrary and changed at Martinmas.

The best workers strode out confidently. Their reputations went before them and they knew they would be hired before nightfall on this first day of the market.

The halflins, those young lads eagerly looking for a first 'fee', as the contract of employment was known, laughed and joked to hide their nervousness.

What if no-one wanted them? How would they look after Mam and Granny and the bairns, if they could not send a few shilling back home now and again?

And some walked, shoulders bowed against the blows that would come, because they knew – and those who would employ them knew – that they had travelled to Forfar because it was the only place where they would be likely to be hired ... by a bad employer, most like, on a poor farm.

Forfar was known as the Rogues' Market, because after the good and the not-so-good were hired, there was still a fee waiting for even the most dubious worker.

Every farmer, horseman and orraman in the east coast of Scotland knew the worth of every other of their kind and it was impossible to hide a tarnished reputation.

At the market town of Forfar, though, it was possible for the desperate to hire the desperate.

The good men would string the farmers along, knowing full well who would hire them before the end of the day, but astute enough to make mileage out of eagerness. There was a good drink or two in it, after all!

And the farmers knew the game and played, too.

But the bad farmer and the bad workman played no games. They just waited dourly till the end of the market days to see who was left to hire and who was hiring.

The mist lay in the valley and hid the town. It was a perfect covering for an imagined fairy kingdom or for phantoms, but Forfar was there all right, the experienced men assured the novices.

Soon, the sun would burn off the mist, and maybe even the very real ghost that did lurk there – the dark spectre of unemployment...

Angus Campbell did not have to set out from his comfortable farmhouse before daybreak. In fact, he had arrived the night before, bringing with him his wife, Lizzie.

It was the first time they had been away together since their wedding trip eight years before. His plan to combine business and pleasure had not been a success, however.

'When you said we'd have a day or two away together, Angus Campbell, I thought you meant in Pitlochry – not in Forfar, just so that you could be first in with a bid on Tam Laird!'

'Ach, Lizzie, don't be like that. It's a night away fae the bairns after all. Come on, lass, we've worked hard for eight years. In five years' time, there'll be a brand-new century.

'If I hire Tam Laird, we'll hae the best horseman in Scotland and when that new century starts I'll take you on a proper holiday, like I promised.'

Reluctantly, Lizzie had agreed to wait, but she had claimed to have a headache when

Angus had invited her to dine elegantly in the hotel dining-room and had made do with a bowl of soup – 'not near as good as my own' – in their room.

She had been snoring softly when Angus had returned upstairs after a meal that he would never confess had not measured up to one of Lizzie's cooking.

Still, she was happier this morning and prepared to be pampered by enjoying breakfast in her room – an indulgence the severely-overworked landlady had agreed to only after a large gratuity had changed hands.

'My wife hasn't been well this past year or so,' Angus had explained. 'A wee bit spoiling now and again does women and good horses no harm...'

And the hostess, who had never been so indulged, had sniffed disparagingly but taken the coins nevertheless and hidden them in her apron.

Relieved that he had done all he could, Angus strode out to the market place with a firm tread. Things had been bad between him and Lizzie since wee James's birth.

It had been a long and difficult confinement and the doctor said Lizzie was afraid to go through all that again ... so, physically, their marriage had been loveless for some time.

Still things would get better. Angus knew

they would – especially if he could hire Tam Laird. That would be the first step to turning the farm around, to making it known all over the east of Scotland.

The men all stood around in groups, corn stalks, signifying that they were for hire, either between their teeth or in their buttonholes.

Tam was at the centre of an admiring crowd. He stood easily, his slight body rock hard in his best suit. He had no straw. Everyone knew that Tam Laird could work for the queen at Balmoral if he told her he was available.

He worked only for a boss he respected and had nearly broken Jake Tullow's jaw a couple of weeks ago after he had caught Jake beating a young horse.

Yes, Tam Laird could pick and choose his employer...

Angus had decided that he would have Tam, whatever the cost. The horseman had worked for him once before and had stayed for two terms – only a year – and somehow his going was bound up in Angus's mind with the unsatisfactory state of his marriage.

Maybe if Tam comes back, he thought, irrationally, Lizzie will love me again.

His incongruous thoughts, and those of every man near him, were interrupted by the sudden arrival of a tinker's cart...

It was driven by a stunning-looking girl, whose large, dark eyes flashed in a beautiful oval face of alabaster whiteness.

Her thick, black, lustrous hair escaped from its red ribbon and blew around her face at the caprice of the wind. She drew up before the group of men whose tweed clothes showed they were farmers.

Was she aware that straws had fallen from mouths, that jaws had dropped open, that all conversation had stopped on her arrival? If she was, she gave no sign.

Lightly, she jumped from the cart. 'Rowena MacFarlane, gentlemen!' she exclaimed, introducing herself. 'This cart and the horse are for sale. I am not. I'm for hire, though – for inside or out.

'I can tend poultry, milk cows, help with the harvest, and I bake bannocks that float from the table if they're not held down with good butter!'

More than one man licked his lips – and not only at the thought of new-baked bannocks – but one coarse farmer spat in the dirt at her feet.

'Irish tinker!' he muttered disparagingly.

She ignored him. 'Actually, I'm Romany,' she said to the others. 'Descended from kings.'

Angus looked at her and acknowledged that Rowena MacFarlane was beautiful, but he thought mainly of Lizzie – Lizzie who

13

was still weak from James's birth and who tired after only a few hours on her feet.

'My wife needs a willing lass to help her,' he said quickly. 'She pays six guineas a year, all found, a dress and two aprons.'

Rowena looked at him from out of her deep, dark eyes. 'A dress fit for the kirk?' she asked in that strange accent that resembled nothing he had ever heard before, not Scots, not Irish.

Perhaps she was a gypsy. Was that what she'd meant by Romany?

'Ay,' he agreed, without thinking of what Lizzie might say.

'My arle?' Rowena asked about the small token of good intent that would formally seal their bargain.

'Half a crown.'

She held out a shapely, sunburned hand and he put the coin in it.

She took it, laughed up at him from beneath her long dark lashes, and bit it between strong, white teeth.

''Tis a deal, Maister,' she said. 'You'll no' want my cart? Right, I'll go and sell it and the beast and meet you back here later.

'That'll be fine, won't it? You'll give me till the end of the day to sell my goods?'

He almost agreed and then remembered that he was master and no servant would dictate to him.

'I have a man to hire and I'll leave before

dinner. You'll be ready then,' he said and she bobbed him a slight curtsy, acknowledging his authority.

Tam Laird, too, had seen Rowena Mac-Farlane and, unconsciously, he had straightened his stance. She was a tall girl, while he was not above middle height.

Tam had worked on farms all over the Mearns and Forfarshire for over 20 years and many feminine lures had been cast in his direction. Tam was no saint and had been more than happy to be hooked now and again – but not landed for good!

He had not yet seen a woman who interested him nearly as much as a good horse did.

Until today…

This filly, he thought, is different. Her beauty and boldness are obvious but there's a gentleness in her, too. She has survived in a hard world, but her spirit's unbroken.

What a pleasure it would be to gentle her, though, to win that proud heart.

The grieve to the Laird of Pitmuir asked Tam to take a drink with him and Angus overheard his offer of employment and worried while Tam pretended to consider it.

Tam had spotted Angus Campbell and knew him for a good employer, an honest, God-fearing man.

Had he not taken a fee at Springhill Farm

when he had first moved down from Aberdeen? But he would not show his willingness to be hired again.

Until Rowena MacFarlane had driven into the market, he had not been completely sure where he intended to rest his head.

Now, with blinding clarity, he knew exactly where he wanted to go, but realised it would not do to appear too eager.

He moved over to where a recruiting sergeant, crimson-jacketed and beribboned with medals, stood extolling the virtues of service in Her Majesty's army.

'Come along, likely lads. Your country needs good strong men to defend her against the foe.

'Take the Queen's shilling, lads – join the army, see the world... Heard of darkest Africa? Well, why not see it for yourself in a fine red coat like mine?'

'Might get killed by the Boers in darkest Africa, General!' an old head yelled.

'You'd die a hero,' the sergeant replied. 'Think of your old mother's pride.'

'She hasnae got any!'

'Will I really get a jacket like yours, General?'

'I'm a sergeant, laddie. Sergeants are a darned sight more important than generals! Yes, I personally guarantee you'll get a jacket and your own rifle, excellent food and accommodation.

'We pay your way to Africa – or India, lad, if you likes tigers – and a wage into the bargain.'

Tam watched as two halflins went off to seal their bargain with him. Who was to know whether or not they were right? They had exchanged one kind of drudgery for another, one hard master for another.

'I'll stick with my Clydesdales,' he muttered under his breath and thought again of Rowena.

'Hello, Mr Campbell. And how are things on the Golden Mile?'

Angus Campbell's land was on that fertile stretch of the Tay between Carnoustie and Arbroath, the Golden Mile, where it seemed to the uninitiated that no work was needed to make things grow and prosper.

'Tam! Good to see you! Look, I won't spin you a line. You're a good horseman – the best maybe – and I came here because I heard you were looking to change jobs.'

'Ay, I am.'

'Well, I've a new bothy built. You'd have your ain bed, dresser, meal chest, a fireplace – oh, ay, and a wash-stand and basin. It's a first-class hotel, Tam!

'I'll pay you a wee bit more than the going weekly rate.'

'You've kept Fern?'

Angus smiled. He should have known that Tam had little interest in his living conditions, or his wage. It was the horses that motivated him, especially Fern, the fine young Clydesdale mare Tam himself had delivered.

'She's in foal to Gavin's Boy.'

'I'd be the *first* horseman at Springhill, I take it?'

'Of course, and I've bought more land, Tam. We have two fine wee laddies now, you see.

'I'll want to leave a nice bit land to each of them.'

Tam had never been interested in children. Somehow, though, today the thought of two wee laddies running behind his plough was pleasant.

'You're offering an arle?'

'Ay, and you'll get it today, right in the palm of your hand, Tam – no waiting till settling day. Five whole shillings I'm offering you.'

Five shillings! It was generous, but no more than Tam had expected. He knew his worth. Before they left the market, he would buy some good tobacco.

'Right, I'll seal the bargain with you, Maister,' he said and they shook hands. Then they went to find an ale wife and maybe a pie man with something savoury for the ale to wash down...

Lizzie Campbell was delighted when her

husband told her that he had hired a woman to live permanently in the house and to help her. She felt that she had aged 20 years in the past eight.

Her slender waist, of which she had once been so proud, had lost its tightness after Colin's birth and had not had time to recover before the arrival of wee James.

And it was no use for a man to tell his crying wife that he thought she was as bonny as she had ever been. Her mirror didn't hide the truth and it told her that she had grown almost stout.

Her light-brown hair was streaked with grey and there were fine lines and often dark shadows around her eyes.

As for her hands, which she had once pampered with creams and lotions...

Well, there was no time for creams when there were men to be fed, babies to be changed, bread to be baked, eggs to be collected and, and, and...

No wonder she was so weary.

But now Angus had hired a country girl to help her. Oh, the bliss of having the fires lit before she even got up in the morning!

If the girl did nothing else, she would do that, and maybe see to the hens, silly creatures that got under her feet when she went to collect the eggs.

She could take James away, too, to give her some time for her first born, her darling

Colin, who had been so neglected of late since sickly James had arrived, demanding all her attention.

Not that she didn't love James, but it would be easier to love him if he did not cling so damply to her 24 hours a day.

Mamma... Lizzie's dear Mamma was looking after her boys just now. Lizzie just knew that for some inexplicable reason James would be calm when she reached home and might even be dry.

She must put on her shawl and bonnet and venture out to the market to buy a gift for Mamma and some gingerbread men for her darling wee boys.

The great range in the kitchen sprung to Lizzie's mind now. The girl could tend to that night and morning, too. That would be a great help.

Feeling better than she had for months, Lizzie Campbell went shopping.

She enjoyed herself thoroughly. She bought gingerbread men and pink sugar mice for the children and found a bolt of cloth that she knew Mamma would love for a new dress.

Perhaps she'd make it up for the New Year.

A tinker sold Lizzie some new porridge spoons, and another one sold her a china jug that would look even more beautiful in the spring when she filled it with wild violets.

She felt so happy that she remembered she had been rather snippety with poor Angus last night and so she went back to the sweetie wife and bought him some treacle toffee, his favourite.

He was a good husband and she had not been much of a wife lately, pushing him away, verbally and physically. But she would try hard to get really well soon. Cuddles and sweet words were a million times better than scolds.

She saw Angus with Tam Laird, a horseman she had known since her childhood. She smiled as she remembered how she and her brother had laughed at the alien speech of the Aberdeenshire halflin her father had hired on an instinct.

'My instinct has never let me down with horses or men,' her dad had said many a time. The last time had been at her wedding breakfast, when he had stood proudly beside his new son-in-law.

Lizzie pushed the cloud of sadness away. Tragically, her father had never seen Colin, the grandson named for him.

'Well, Tam Laird,' she said, 'I hear you're coming back to Springhill Farm.'

Tam pushed his bunnet a little farther back on his head and then pulled it down again, by way of salute. He smiled his shy, crooked smile.

'Ay, Missus. I hear there are two fine

laddies now to help me with the horses.'

'It's the boys that've brought you back to us, is it? Nothing to do with our horses, then?' teased Lizzie, who was feeling better every minute. She had always liked Tam.

Tam never answered her question for, at the moment, Rowena MacFarlane, having disposed of her horse and her cart, came looking for her new employer.

Lizzie Campbell saw her: saw the full figure, the flashing black eyes, the white skin, and the exuberant mane of dark, curling, silky hair.

She was like the wild rose that flung itself wantonly over the wall near the apple orchard – fertile, abundant, abandoned.

Lizzie swallowed hard, but said nothing, not a word, until she and Angus were alone in a private parlour at the Inn.

'So that's the "wee country lassie" tae help me with the bairns, Angus. She's a… She's a…'

'She's just a tinker lass for hire,' Angus said.

'She's a strumpet, you mean – and I'll not have her near my bairns!'

'Och, Lizzie, it's no' like you to condemn somebody because the good Lord chose to give her a pretty face.'

Lizzie rounded on him. 'So, you agree she's pretty!'

Angus thought swiftly, and cunning he did

not know he possessed, came to his aid.

'Have I not been living with the prettiest woman in the county for eight years? Of course I can see she's pretty, for them that likes the full-blown rose.

'But what I really see, Lizzie, is a pair of strong arms that can take some of the load off my wee pet and hopefully put some of the roses back in her cheeks.'

She was appeased. 'Oh, Angus, I know I haven't been a good wife lately and I will try to do better.'

'And Rowena will be there to help you.'

Her softness vanished again. 'Rowena? What kind of a heathen name is that? Rowena! She's named after a tree!'

'Lassie, I don't care what she's named as long as I can get hame to my farm with Tam Laird on the back of my cart.

'There'll be a dance the nicht in Springhill that they'll be talking about for generations!

'They'll say, "do ye mind o' the dance they had when auld Angus hired Tam Laird?" And you'll be there showing them how to reel!'

But Lizzie was suddenly tired again and all she wanted to do was get home to her babies and her mother, who would surely cosset her just one more night – and let her go to bed before the start of what would certainly be the wildest party for many a long day...

Perhaps the mistress of Springhill Farm should have made the effort to attend the party.

Wee James, happy for once, his face pink both with exertion and sugar mice, demanded to be taken to the new bothy to see the fiddlers tuning up.

His father perched him on the top of a kist with dire threats of what he would do to him if he got in the way, and the toddler sat there obediently, starry eyed, and watched the preparations.

The fiddlers, two of them, and a man with a mandolin, another with the bagpipes, prepared to play the night away.

Kegs of ale were rolled down from the house, where a huge boiler of skirlie, that favourite and inexpensive dish of onions and oatmeal fried in fat, was put on the back of the ever-lit stove to keep warm.

The beds and the kists, or chests – including the one on which the wide-eyed James sat – were pushed to the walls to leave plenty of room for the dancing, and every utensil that could possibly be used for the consumption of liquid was unearthed and given a cursory wipe.

Wee James saw auld Harry Begg, the ploughman, wipe his mug on the back of his trews and, the very next day, he was absolutely shocked when his mother slapped his legs for trying the same trick!

He was taken home by his father long before the fun really started, but he was dandled in time to the music by every one of the men, and by the new lassie, Rowena, when she came down from the house after helping his granny tidy it up for the morning.

'He wears a blue bonnet, blue bonnet, blue bonnet,' Rowena sang, and Angus was not the only man who admired her strong voice and the rounded softness of her arms as the little boy bobbed up and down on her red-skirted lap.

Angus had not intended to return to the bothy after he carried his two-year-old back to the house.

Lizzie, encouraged by her mother, had gone to bed soon after she had read Colin a story, and was almost asleep when her husband brought her the child.

'I'm too tired,' Lizzie pleaded. 'Have the new lass put James to bed. That's why we hired her, isn't it?'

And so Angus had strolled back down to the bothy and arrived in time to see Rowena whirl past him in Tam Laird's arms. He was not the only man watching her.

Some of the bothy lads were being daft and dancing with one another, but most sat and guzzled as much of the ale as they could, while their hungry eyes devoured the beautiful girl.

Angus looked at the girl and saw her assess him boldly – woman to man, not employee to master. He stared back, feeling suddenly unsteady as he looked into the girl's exotic, dark eyes.

He had had too much to drink – and he was not used to strong ale...

Time to stop this, he thought angrily. He caught at Tam's arm as they skipped past him again and, to his chagrin, realised that both Tam and the girl thought he was intending to take Tam's place in the dance.

Suddenly the thought of dancing with a beautiful girl in his arms was very appealing. Lizzie had been as light as a feather once, not so long ago. No, he chastised himself – this won't do...

'There's a tired wee laddie sitting with his granny in the scullery,' he said coldly. 'There'll be plenty of time for dancing when he's in his crib.'

'Ay, and bring the skirlie with you when you come back, lass,' called one of the older men as Rowena went off towards the farmhouse.

'We'll hae tae find a man for that one, Maister Campbell,' said John Smith, the second horseman, 'and quick, or we'll hae every red-blooded man in Forfarshire sniffin' at the door!'

'Well, there's Tam,' Angus said moodily, as

he mentally pulled himself together.

The old man laughed. 'Tam Laird? There's no' a woman alive who'll come as near tae him as his blinkin' horses!'

Agreeing, Angus suddenly felt exultant. Yes! Yes! He had done it! He had hired Tam Laird!

'You're ab-abs-olutely right, John,' he slurred. 'Come on, lads, one more drink to welcome Tam home, and then I'm away to my bed.'

He deserved to crow about his good fortune, did he not? Three other farmers had been after Tam but *he* had got him.

Angus stayed long enough to take a drink or two more than he should have with the men and to talk to Tam about the Clydesdale, Fern, who was due to drop her foal soon.

He did not mean to meet Rowena in the yard. He did not mean to take the heavy boiler of skirlie from her: he would scarce have thought of carrying a pot for Lizzie.

There were jobs women did, like cleaning and cooking and having babies, and there were jobs that men did...

But the girl had had a long, stressful day, and there were dark circles around her eyes, shadows that somehow added to her beauty, to the tempting promises that were in her eyes, her lips.

'No. No! You'll no' be much use to your

mistress if you get too tired, lass,' he said softly, as he refused to listen to her protestations and took the pot from her.

She was, as Tam had noted, a fighter.

'I don't tire easy,' she said with a defiant toss of her head and her thick hair brushed his cheek, which was enough to start the blood pounding in his veins.

'Give us a jig, lads!' he called when, to his men's astonishment, he walked back into the bothy carrying the huge pan of hot food.

The fiddlers began to play – toe-tapping music.

Angus put the boiler on the table and told Tam to start serving. Then he turned and caught Rowena by the arm.

'Let's see how easily you tire,' he whispered and began to whirl her around the room.

She laughed boldly into his eyes, while she relaxed in his arms and everything and everyone except Rowena MacFarlane disappeared from Angus's mind.

The fiddlers called a halt first.

'Come on, Maister Campbell, give us a break. I've a thirst on me like a pilgrim in a desert!'

Breathless, Angus came laughingly and a little unsteadily to a halt.

'Well, lads,' he called to the orramen and halflins, 'now you know how it's done! You should be ashamed an auld man like me has tae show you where tae set your feet in a dance!'

He did not look again at Rowena as he accepted yet another mug of ale from Tam.

'Will you hae some skirlie, Maister?' Tam asked. 'Or a puffie-tootie?'

Angus smiled as he looked down at the plate of fancy cakes that his mother-in-law had baked and sent down for the celebration. He was glad that they had been well hidden from wee James.

'Dear me, no, Tam. I had my tea cooked by Mistress Gillies,' he said. 'I'm too full even for a wee cake!'

Why on earth, he thought, had his mother-in-law made such daft-like wee cakes for great hungry men? Still, it had been a thoughtful gesture.

He only wished Lizzie had inherited more of her mother's talents. But that thought was disloyal and he dismissed it.

He had had far too much to drink and needed some clear, sweet air. He set down his beer mug and made for the door and it's doubtful if many of the men saw him go: they were far too engrossed in the unaccustomed food and drink to worry about their employer.

And even on a farm like Springhill, where the boss did some hands-on work and was seen on most days by his employees, it was the grieve – the gaffer – that they feared,

29

not the farmer.

Bothy life was hard and there were few causes for celebration. They had New Year's Day off and the market days and that was about it, unless there was some private joy, like a wedding.

In the spring and summer, when the days were long, the men worked all the hours of daylight and returned to the bothies only to eat and sleep.

In winter, of course, they had more time to amuse themselves, but this was almost summer and an extra, unexpected party had to be savoured. And it was.

Angus heard the shouts and the laughter as he sat on a wall smoking a last pipe and he rejoiced that he had so easily made his hard-working people so happy.

He was responsible for them, for his three horsemen, his two orramen or general labourers, the two halflins who were, he thought, scarcely dry behind the ears.

Then there were the wives of his grieve, of one of the horsemen, and of an orraman, all of whom had their wee houses on his land, where they raised their children.

He liked to see children running about the place, playing merrily in the dirt with his own two.

Now he was also responsible for the well-being of Rowena MacFarlane.

Romany or tinker, what did it matter? She

was a woman on her own.

And what a woman!

The bothy where the party was being held was modern and had a window and from where he sat he could see her sometimes.

She was a beautiful creature and the single men would be very happy to flirt with her – and more – given half a chance.

She'd better be as capable of doing as good a day's work as she boasted, he told himself angrily, as he emptied his tobacco on to the ground at his feet.

But still he sat on in the twilight, telling himself he was enjoying that pale, blue-grey light that was so much a part of a late evening in Forfarshire.

He watched his cattle move against it, they grazed contentedly on the late spring's lush grass, and then he stood up as Rowena walked softly towards him across the yard.

She said nothing when she reached him, but her eyes, her great dark eyes, held his gaze and mirrored his own deep, uncontrollable desires...

Angus looked down at her sensual charms and was lost as his mouth covered hers.

'Romany or witch?' he whispered, as he took her hand and pulled her eagerly into the great barn.

The summer was beautiful: how blue the sky, how white the little clouds that scudded along on windy days or drifted languorously in the heat.

Crops seemed to thrust themselves eagerly from the ground, stood swaying gracefully as they changed from green to gold and then bowed their ripe heads under the reapers' sickles.

Under Rowena's tolerant, watchful eye, wee James grew stronger and healthier, too, and was soon running, as brown as a berry, with his brother.

Tam had them underfoot most often for they shared his passion for the horses and loved nothing more than to be tossed like sacks of grain on to a broad brown back.

The harvest was a good one and was completed before the cold winds blew in, driving the summer before them and pulling autumn along in their wake.

Angus sat by his fire with his pipe and congratulated himself on the soundness of his judgment.

He'd been right. Everything had improved from the day Tam Laird had come back to his farm.

'Can I hae a word with you, Maister?' How quickly Rowena, the kitchen deem, the maid he had hired at Whitsun, had adopted the speech patterns of the other workers.

Lizzie was often heard scolding her for she had plans for her sons and did not want them to speak like the 'common' workers.

Colin was a clever boy.

Lizzie intended to cajole Angus into sending him to a fee-paying school in Dundee.

Startled, Angus looked up at Rowena and then turned his eyes away.

Since that fateful night, he had avoided her as much as he could. That was easy enough in the summer when he could work in the fields until she was tucked up safely in her wee room off the kitchen.

'I have to talk to you.'

The despair in her voice chilled Angus. He had almost convinced himself that their liaison had not happened, that he had dreamed it. And now she was looking at him with great eyes so that he was compelled to look again.

Her hands were held protectively across her middle. She had put on weight since she had come to work for Lizzie and had taken to wearing looser clothing.

All that good fresh farm food, he supposed... Or–

'Oh, my God!' He stood up quickly and she shied away almost fearfully.

'Tell me it's not true,' he implored.

Her fear left her then and she was Rowena again – proud, defiant and beautiful.

'I'm to hae a baby, Maister – *your* baby.'

The great stallion stood patiently while his mane and tail were plaited, while his coat was curried and brushed till it shone.

The small boy sitting astride him bent over and breathed on as much of the broad back as he could reach without pitching off on to the ground far, far below.

Then he rubbed with his cloth as ferociously as his puny strength would allow.

Rowena, he had noticed, breathed on Mammy's best spoons before she wiped them and put them away in the drawer. So, if hot breath was good for silver, surely it could do no harm to a magnificent big Clydesdale?

Tam Laird looked up at wee Jamie Campbell's glowing, red face and smiled quietly to himself.

Colin, being that bit older, was much more useful as a groom, but it did the younger of the laddies no harm to feel as though he, too, was helping. One day, with encouragement, he would do a grand day's work.

'That's a fine polish you're putting on Gavin's Boy's withers, Jamie lad. We're sure to pick up a winner's rosette after a' the work you and Colin have put in.'

Colin stopped his work and looked up at Tam. 'Is that true, Tam? You're no' just sayin' that to make us feel good, are you?'

Tam picked him up and dumped him on the horse beside his wee brother.

'Me, tell fibs? Away wi' you! You're the two best ornamen on this farm and that's the truth.

'If … *when* the judge pins that rosette on Gavin's Boy, I'll no' know which of you to give it to. Maybe I could pin the two of you thegither wi' it!'

At the thought of being joined together by a fine blue rosette, the two boys giggled uproariously.

To them, Tam Laird was wonderful. They loved him more than anyone in the whole world … except Mammy and Daddy, of course – and maybe Rowena, who never smacked them like Mammy and was never too busy to play.

Even with her arms deep in soap suds at the Monday wash, Rowena could be counted on to blow bubbles all over them.

'Weena!' Spotting the maid, Jamie wobbled precariously on his perch and Tam automatically put up a strong, callused hand to hold him steady.

Looking in the direction of the child's urgent waving, he saw Rowena heading across the yard with a clothes-basket on her hip.

She heard Jamie's cry and lifted one arm to return his wave and suddenly all Tam's suspicions of the past few weeks were confirmed.

As Rowena balanced the heavy basket, her skirts clung to her and her figure was clearly outlined. Her swollen belly told its own tale. She *was* with child!

The disappointment was almost painful. Until now, Tam would have argued with any of the other men that young Rowena MacFarlane would remain virtuous.

'Ach, for all her fine airs, she's nothin' but a tinker lassie, and nae better than she should be!'

That was one remark he'd overheard in the bothy, but Tam had put it down to simple jealousy.

'Well, I'm no' the faither,' said one of the lads, 'and it's no' auld Harry and I doubt if young Josh would have the nerve to even talk to her – so who is it?'

Tam knew all about mares and he knew everything there was to know about foaling. Women were less familiar territory, but for all that, he did some rapid mental arithmetic on dates and came up with an answer he did not like.

He picked up the huge horse collar that he had rubbed with blacking and beeswax. He had used a beetle, a strong stick, to rub in the polish. The metal pieces had been scoured with emery paper until they sparkled and the collar looked fit for a prizewinner.

Tam looked down at Gavin's Boy's huge feet. How white they looked against the dark brown of his great legs. One part of his mind was admiring the horse, thinking how useful it was to have one with white feet: it helped a horseman see his way home on dark, winter evenings.

The rest of his mind was racing with painful thoughts of Rowena.

I cannae believe it... She must have fallen pregnant afore she even came to us.

And then he asked himself the biggest, hardest question of all.

What, in the name of goodness, is she going to do now?

At first, Lizzie Campbell had thoroughly enjoyed having a girl like Rowena Mac-Farlane in her household. Rowena was more than a kitchen deem, a kitchen maid.

She was a cook, a nursemaid, a seam-stress, even, yes, a friend.

She worked in or out in all weathers with unfailing good humour and no matter how tired she must sometimes have been – yes, Lizzie occasionally conceded that, at times, Rowena had too much to do – she was always ready to take the boys away to bathe them, or to insist that her mistress put her well-shod feet up, while she made her a cup of hot, sweet tea.

Everything in the farmhouse had improved beyond recognition in the months since Angus had hired the girl. Lizzie herself was more even tempered.

She was sleeping better, mainly since wee James no longer girned and whined all day.

With Rowena to do all ... to do a *share* of the work ... she had even found time to go back to her fine sewing. Angus liked to see her sitting by the window, an embroidery frame in her hands, when he came home at the end of a long day.

That was all men really wanted, a comfortable home, a pretty wife, quiet, clean children, and a good meal on the table the moment they stepped through the door.

'How did I manage before Rowena came?' Lizzie had asked herself more than once.

She was not quite sure when she began to have her disturbing suspicions, vague concerns that made her eye Rowena carefully, looking ... looking for what?

No, Lizzie was a good woman, a well-brought-up woman. She would try to dismiss the nightmarish worry that niggled at her increasingly...

Angus Campbell, too, was quite delighted with the results of his visit to the Feein' Market.

At first...

Tam Laird had settled in as if he had never been away and was bringing along the young horses and the two new lads gently and firmly.

And Rowena?

Deliberately, Angus had turned his thoughts away from the madness of that May night when he had been intoxicated by the sweet scent of hawthorn and by too much ale.

It had seemed to work out all right. Lizzie had forgiven Rowena for her heathen strangeness, and even, it seemed, for her beauty.

Thank goodness beauty fades, Angus had thought often as he had watched Rowena attend to her tasks.

If she stayed with them for five years, at least till the bairns were out from under Lizzie's feet, he was sure that he would no longer see the exotic, untamed creature who had captivated his senses on that fateful evening.

But now, after her horrifying announcement about her pregnancy, his usually quick mind had let him down, turned sluggish.

He laughed wryly to himself as he reflected that at one time he had believed that the new, soft, gentle beauty Rowena had acquired lately was simply due to the good food she ate at his table!

He prayed silently, as he finished his work for the day, that a solution could be found before everyone in the world knew about her condition...

When he arrived home, Lizzie was not in her chair by the window as usual. He was surprised and vaguely uneasy. Real ladies did embroidery and his Lizzie liked to think of herself, not as the wife of a working farmer, but as a grand lady.

And so you will be, one day, my Lizzie, he said to himself, as he climbed the stairs to the family bedrooms.

Lizzie must be taking a turn at telling the boys their bedtime story. That was it, of course. That's what she'd be doing.

He might be in time to join in. Colin liked to hear his father's deep voice pretending to be the characters in the fairy stories.

As it happened, Lizzie was standing at the window in their bedroom, but he could feel the heat of her anger from the other side of the room.

'Lizzie?'

'I warned you about her, Angus Campbell, but you wouldn't listen! Oh, no! You stupid men always know best, don't you?'

Dear heaven, she had found out, even although Rowena had sworn that nothing would show for a month or two yet!

Give me a little more time, he prayed silently. Please Lord, just a little more happy time. Things had been so good lately. Lizzie had been her old sweet, loving self.

'Lizzie?' he said again and this time she turned from the window and he saw the rage in her eyes.

'I told you that slut was no good! I told you I didn't want her near my bairns! But, oh no, you said I was to show her Christian charity.

'Well, somebody on this farm has been showing that, that—' she could not bring herself to say the word that hovered on the tip of her tongue '–that *woman* a lot more than charity and I want them both off my land tomorrow!'

His mind refused to grasp what she was telling him and, instead, took refuge in land ownership.

'The farm belongs to the baith of us, Lizzie. That was your faither's will. He wanted us to inherit equal shares. "A wee bit lassie cannae own a farm" ... that's what he always said.'

'*My* farm, *your* farm, *our* farm, call it what you will – but that trollop leaves the place tonight! Do you hear me?'

Angus's knees finally gave up the battle to support him and he sank down on to the four-poster bed.

'Trollop, you say?'

'Ay, your precious Rowena! She's having a bairn, Angus. I don't expect you to have noticed: you never even knew when *I* was carrying, but she is.

'When I think of that hussy carrying on here, right under my nose, while she played with my innocent laddies…

'Well, she's in the vegetable patch just now picking sprouts. You get out there and tell her to leave!'

His mouth was dry and his heart was thudding in his chest. Not yet. There had to be a way out of this. But he could see no option other than to brazen it out.

'Lizzie, Lizzie, calm down! She can't be … what you say. She can't be.'

'She is, Angus! I've been wonderin' for a few weeks now. She's getting thicker around the middle and bigger…' She stopped herself, embarrassed. '…Well, you know, up top. Ay, and her eyes are white and clear.'

'That's a sure sign, my mother says. She knew when I fell with our Colin because of the whites of my eyes.'

Lizzie grabbed her husband and almost pulled him, big as he was, from the bed. 'So you get out there and tell that gypsy hussy to pack her bags. I want her out of here – now!'

Angus felt devastated. It had happened. It had happened. And it was all his fault.

Desperately, he tried to force his terrified mind to come up with some kind of solution.

He turned to his wife and took her in his arms.

'Sweetheart, Lizzie, if what you're sayin' is true and Rowena has made a mistake ... well, she's no' the first lassie to be caught and she'll definitely no' be the last.

'In the name of Christian charity, we cannae just put her out. Where's she going to go? It's November, lass, a month afore Christmas. You cannae throw a lassie on to the streets a few weeks afore Christmas.'

Lizzie stood by her dressing-table and began to pull pins out of her hair.

'Just watch me!' she yelled. 'You've aye been soft, Angus. Well, if you're not man enough to tell her, I damn well will!'

'Or I'll get the minister to hac a word wi' you. He'll tell you all about Christian charity. It begins at home, Angus Campbell, with your wife and your wee boys.'

The minister. No, no, everything would come out. Rowena would tell the truth and then there where would he be? Where would his marriage be, his reputation in the community?

Was he not an elder of the kirk, the first man in his family to attain that office, an honour and responsibility of which – apart from that moment of summer madness – he had always tried to be worthy?

'All right, all right, I'll talk to Rowena, Lizzie,' he began desperately. 'Maybe,

43

maybe the man'll marry her.'

Oh, how those words choked him. The man? *He* was the man. How could he marry her? His marriage, his farm, his personal standards were dissolving before his very eyes.

'I'll talk to her,' he repeated.

Angus went out, leaving Lizzie to tightly close the window against the cold evening air, and met Tam Laird in the steading.

'Well, Tam,' he said.

'Evening, Maister. Were you wanting something, for I'm away tae groom Fern? The bairns have been helping me get Gavin's Boy ready for the show. We're going to win that rosette this year, you mark my words.'

Tam looked at his employer shrewdly. There was something wrong at the house. Everybody in the bothy had heard the loud yelling from the bedroom.

My, but the mistress could shout like a fishwife when the spirit moved her. She had found out about Rowena and, like most virtuous women, wanted rid of her, no doubt.

Let he who is without sin cast the first stone. The words from the good book echoed in Tam's head.

But then the mistress never sinned.

'Tam...' his employer said again and the

44

horseman waited patiently for him to compose himself and gather his thoughts.

'Ay, Maister,' he said quietly, when it was embarrassingly obvious that Angus was finding it impossible to speak.

'Tam,' Angus started again. Then, taking a deep breath, he decided to be bold, 'Tam, Mrs Campbell tells me that things are no' weel with her kitchen deem.'

'Rowena?'

'Ay, Rowena.'

Damn it, he had to do better than repeat everything that was said, but the acid juices were still churning in his stomach. 'Would you know anything about her, em, condition, Tam?'

There, he had said it. He was a lecher and a liar, and he knew better than anybody that Tam was innocent, but he had to save his marriage.

Never ever had these acres, that stone farmhouse, those wee laddies been more precious to him.

'It's no' the end of the world, Tam, man tae man. She'd still make someone,' he stared deep into his first horseman's eyes, 'a fine, bonny wife.'

Tam looked at him. 'There was a time when I might hae been glad to take that lass on, Maister, but no' now. She's spoiled goods. You'll hae tae look elsewhere.

'And I doubt if her condition has onything

to do with this ferm. Think about it. Auld Harry's past it; John cannae abide her – thinks she's nothin' but a no-good tinker – and Josh is scared o' her.

'She just has to look at him and he's useless for the rest of the day!'

Was this a way out? Was Tam, in his innocence, his goodness, call it what you will, handing him an answer?

'You mean, Tam, that you're not the father and no-one else in the bothy is capable?'

'Well, there's capable and there's available, Maister, and they're two very different things. Rowena's stuck close by the farm, even on her time off. There's been no nonsense around here, I'm pretty sure of that.

'She must have lain wi' some man afore she came here. It's obvious.'

Thank God, Angus thought, relieved. That's what they would all think. That's what everyone would believe. No-one would listen to Rowena, even if she were to say anything.

I swear I'll make it all right for her and her bairn, he silently promised whatever deity was listening.

'Poor lass,' he said now and his flesh crawled at his hypocrisy. 'What are we going to do, Tam?'

Tam looked at him in surprise. The woman's problem was none of his making:

46

he saw no reason to help her solve it.

Angus knew fine well what was going through the horseman's head.

'It's the mistress, Tam. She's guessed the truth. Women know about these things, goodness knows how. But the bottom line is she's all for throwing Rowena out – and winter's coming…'

'Well, at least she'll have a few pence put by – she sold her horse and cart at the Feein' Market, mind. You'll forgive my bold speaking, Maister, but you cannae be held responsible for Rowena just because you gave her a job.

'I doubt you'd have hired her if you'd known what kind of lassie she was.'

'I don't see her as a bad lassie, Tam. Where's the evidence?'

'Are you kiddin'? In aboot three months' time there'll be the noisiest scrap of evidence you'd ever want tae see, Maister!

'Well, if there's nothing else, I'll, em, bid you goodnight. I've a horse waiting to be seen to.'

Desperately, Angus turned.

'And when you've finished with the horse, Tam, what's waiting? A hard bed in a bothy with an auld man and a witless loon for company!

'How can that compare with the joy of going home to Rowena? As a married man, you'd be entitled to a place of your own.'

Tam cast his mind back to the first time he'd seen Rowena – the glorious, proud creature on the wagon, and his heart stirred.

Fancy going home to such a woman; to his own wee cottage; to his own fireside; to his own bed...

Then harsh reality stepped in to banish the imagined idyll.

'I'd sooner do without than pick up some other man's leavings, Maister!'

So saying, he touched his cap and calmly walked off to the stable.

Angus watched him go. For a desperate moment, he had felt sure that Tam would solve his dilemma by offering to take the woman's hand. He had almost heard the fiddler's wild music for the wedding dance.

Some other man's leavings. It was he, Angus Campbell, who had reduced Rowena to being thought of like that. And the child she was carrying was his – as much his as Colin and wee James were.

And, for the first time, he felt anger towards the mother of this unborn child. He had not forced her to lie with him. She had bewitched him with her soft voice and her beautiful, dark eyes...

This mess was all Rowena's fault, he thought vehemently. She could drown in a ditch for all he cared ... but the child...

'Were you looking for me, Maister?'

Angus had not seen her walk towards him with the pot of brussels sprouts in her hand and instantly regretted his cruel, unreasonable thoughts.

'I heard the shouting fae your house – in fact, the hale of Forfarshire must have heard!' she added with a harsh laugh. 'I take it my secret's out. Will you be callin' the meenister in to talk to me about the sins of the flesh?'

'Listen, are you sure this child is mine?' he asked angrily, remembering Tam's words.

Then he saw by the scornful, disappointed look in her eyes that his question had alienated him forever from the proud mother of his unborn child.

'There's no need for the minister to be involved, Rowena.'

In truth, that was the last thing he wanted. He had to solve this problem himself, but how.

'This mess is of our making. We have to think.'

'I *have* thought. I've told you already. If you can get me a month's grace, less maybe, I'll be gone. Neither the bairn nor me will be a burden on you. Your reputation will not be tarnished, I promise you that.'

'But where will you go? If you say nothing, Rowena, I'll always be grateful. I'll never forget you ... or the child. The bairn is mine,' – his voice was sincere – 'and I have a duty towards it. I'll support it, never turn my back on it. That's my promise.'

Rowena straightened up and once again she was the proud, free spirit.

He heard her words from the Feein' Market again.

I am for hire ... not for sale...

'I heard your words,' she told Angus now. 'But just you persuade the mistress to leave me be for a few weeks, no more, and I'll never ask you for anything again.'

With that she turned and left him, as if he were the servant and she, the master.

Turning, too, he glanced up at the farmhouse window, to see Lizzie staring down at him, witness to both encounters...

It was young Colin Campbell who first saw the evidence of their coming. He had escaped after his morning porridge and had run, as fast as his bulky winter clothes would allow, to the burn.

The water was so fast and deep since the rains that it made the sailing of make-believe boats an adventure.

The frosts of the past two days had been so hard, though, that it was difficult for his small, frozen fingers to pry the twigs that formed his 'boats' from the soil in which they were embedded.

Jack Frost held them fast, so Colin ran on. He would find a stone soon, or a big stick that would help him release his entrapped fleet.

And then he noticed something else in the rime. Cart tracks. The little boy stopped.

He had been familiar with the ruts made by farm vehicles since he could first put one unsteady foot in front of the other, but these were different.

He forgot all about his armada and ran along inside the unusual tracks.

And then he saw them...

Wagons. Horses. Children. Swarthy men and dark-haired women gathered around open fires. Dogs that ran towards him snapping and snarling.

Though he was only five, Colin knew how to deal with these creatures. He stood firm, realising that their noisy show was mostly bravado.

Besides, a tall man with black, curly hair had seen him and was calling the dogs back, cowed, to their places beneath the wagons.

'Hello, little lord,' the man said and Colin laughed, for his accent sounded just like Rowena's.

'I'm no' a lord!' he giggled. 'I'm just wee Colin.'

'Well, good morning, wee Colin,' the man said again. 'Welcome to my home.'

Colin looked puzzled. How could a field be a home? Home was a strong house with shuttered windows and a door that Daddy bolted at night.

Then he remembered a picture-book that Rowena had shown him. 'Do you live in a wagon?'

'I do – that one there,' the man replied cheerfully, pointing to a wagon with a bright yellow door, carved and painted with strange signs and symbols.

'I wish I lived there!' Colin exclaimed.

The man chuckled then said something in a strange language to an old woman who was sitting on the steps of a wagon. To Colin's astonishment, she was smoking a clay pipe just like Tam or auld Harry!

She stood up and knocked the ashes from her pipe on to the ground. Then she rubbed her hands on the skirts of her dress and held out a hand to Colin.

'Marek, my son, says you're welcome to look inside, young master,' she said. 'You should be honoured! 'Tis not everyone who's invited to step inside the home of a prince.'

Colin stood gaping first at her hand with its gold rings and then back at the man with the curly hair. He was amazed to see that he had a gold ring in one ear. Was that how princes dressed?

'Are you a prince?' Mammy and Rowena had told him stories of princes who lived in castles.

'I am!' The man laughed again and Colin

did too, for the sound was so infectious. It was like Rowena's laugh, and like Rowena, the man showed even white teeth when he smiled.

That was the first thing the boy had noticed about Rowena, her teeth, and then it had been her strange, soft voice, like music.

Colin walked confidently towards the wagon. It was like a caravan in a fairy story and the man was a prince, so if he climbed up those wooden steps, he would be in the fairy story, too.

'Fool!' another voice muttered and one of the women, stirring the contents of a pot, almost sprang forward to stop the lad.

'You're acting like a child yourself, Marek, to think of allowing a bairn inside your wagon!' she chastised. 'He's but a baby and his mother lives nearby. What'll she say when she hears that her child's been inside a "damned tinker's" wagon?'

They spoke heatedly for a few minutes in that strange, foreign tongue and then Marek turned to Colin and there was regret in his voice.

'I'm afraid the woman's quite right, young sir. Unfortunately, we have a bad name, we travellers. Your mother probably wouldn't approve of you being in our camp.'

His voice was gentle, his manner kindly. 'Do you live nearby?'

Colin was deeply disappointed. He did not understand everything the tall man said, but he knew he was not to be allowed to see inside the wonderful painted wagon, after all, and that upset him. For a moment, he thought he might cry like wee James.

He pointed back towards the farmhouse. 'Yes,' he replied, fighting to hold back the tears, 'just over there – at the farm,' he said with a sob.

And, so saying, he turned and ran as fast as he could back to safety and security...

Angus Campbell saw his son rushing into the yard and stopped his work to call to the boy.

'What's up, Colin? Who's chasing you, laddie?' he asked, gathering the youngster up into his arms.

Colin clung to him for a moment before being set down.

'N-nobody,' he said when he had composed himself enough to speak. 'There's wagons, Daddy, beautiful wagons, down by the river, but the man wouldn't let me see inside 'em.'

So the tinkers were back... Well, it was wintertime and, provided no hens went missing, they could stay.

They were good at mending things and although Lizzie would allow them nowhere near the house, she often bought odd items from them, clothes pegs and baskets…

'Colin tells me he's seen tinkers down by the river,' he said to Lizzie some time later, as she spooned hot soup into their bowls at dinner time.

Rowena, sitting quietly in the window recess with her mending – the light was better there – said nothing, but her head lifted momentarily from the shirt she was sewing and she glanced out of the window.

'Tinkers!' Lizzie said viciously. 'Dirty thieves and wastrels! Send them on their way, Angus, and let them take their strumpet here with them.'

Lizzie had been worn down by Angus's arguments and had finally agreed to let Rowena stay on until he could find another maid of all work. For his part, Angus had pledged to find a replacement as quickly as possible.

In the meantime, the 'disgraced' Rowena was supposed to keep well out of sight whenever anyone came to call.

It was not an admirable arrangement, for Lizzie vented her spleen on the maid servant at every opportunity.

Rowena undoubtedly made things worse by saying nothing and looking – defiantly, Lizzie contended – proudly, Angus thought, at her mistress, while Lizzie ranted and raved.

Angus had had no further conversation

with Rowena. Yet it was somehow understood that she was to stay until other arrangements could be made – but what arrangements?

Days were passing and Rowena's condition was becoming more and more obvious. The atmosphere inside the farmhouse grew increasingly explosive, while the year steadily marched on towards the birthday of the Prince of Peace.

On the Sunday before Christmas, the Campbells and all their servants went, as always, to the local church for the morning service.

Lizzie presumed that Rowena would stay at home.

She did not.

As soon as the trap with the family and the cart with the farm servants had disappeared round the corner, Rowena threw her shawl around her shoulders and hurried off to the field by the river, where the tinkers were camped...

'Your problem has been solved, Maister,' she whispered to Angus later that night. 'In two days' time, I'll be gone.'

Puzzled, he looked at her blankly and lifted the oil lamp closer to her face, as if that would make what she had said any clearer.

'Gone? Gone where?'

'Back to my own people. They're Romanies by the way, not tinkers. My people don't judge – they accept. I'll be safe there until the babe is born – and after, if I choose to stay.'

Turning from him, she went down the passage to her room and he stood feeling the cold night air closing around him.

She could not go, not with the gypsies!

He would never see her again if she went with them. He knew that as well as he knew his own name.

'It's for the best,' said a voice within him, but he argued with it. If Rowena went with the gypsies, his child would grow up a vagabond, hounded from town and village, cursed, reviled and feared.

His child. *His* bairn, like the two upstairs in their wee cots.

He could not let that happen. He had to speak to Rowena again, to convince her. He would definitely talk to Tam again, in the New Year maybe, when a drink might make him forget his scruples a wee bit.

If the horseman married Rowena, Angus's child would grow up on the farm. He would see it develop. He'd be able to care for its welfare.

Distraught, he went to start after Rowena, but Lizzie was at the head of the stairs, her hair around her shoulders and a shawl over her nightgown.

'Come up to bed, Angus. What on earth are you doing down there in the dark?'

'Nothing,' he murmured softly. 'I'm doing nothing, Lizzie.'

And that's the shame of it, he thought wearily, as he headed for the stairs. I'm doing nothing to prevent this parting from my unborn child.

Tuesday, December 24, 1895

The wind was blowing from the North and snow threatened. Inside the little church on this icy Christmas Eve, the less devout distracted themselves by watching the drifting, smoke-like patterns their cold breath made as they exhaled.

Angus Campbell was not watching his breath … neither was he praying.

His wife, Lizzie, was beside him in her best coat and hat, her muffler and her fur-lined gloves, and if she was cold, she gave no sign of it. Instead, she sang lustily in her ever-so-slightly out of tune voice.

Sometimes Angus found the sound endearing. At this Watchnight Service, however, it grated on his ears, and on his sadly overwrought nerves.

'Silent night, Holy night.
All is calm. All is bright.'

From the moment he'd been old enough to be taken to the kirk on a Sunday, he'd loved the old carols and the joyful story of Christmas.

But not this year. This year, the only babe he could think about was the one that Rowena MacFarlane, his wife's maid-of-all-work, was expecting.

She was leaving, disappearing with the travelling folk, the tinkers, the gypsies. Call them what you will, the end result would be the same. A child of his making, kin to Colin and James, was going to be brought up like a savage by strange people who spoke in a strange tongue.

And there was nothing he could do about it.

Rowena had known that the gypsies were coming. She had grown up with them. She was an accepted part of the clan, the family, and therefore, she had somehow known. Sixth sense, perhaps ... instinct...

She had accepted a hiring fee from Angus Campbell because she had felt that something in him had spoken to her. It had been, despite their obvious differences, like calling to like.

She had not hired herself into service in Forfarshire because she had known that one day soon, Marek and the tribe would be there. It had not been so that she could show Marek that she could manage, that she did not need him, even though she was now fatherless and alone.

It had not been to show Marek that she did not care about him growing so fond of Romany girl Pheemie Stewart and all her bold ways.

No, the truth was Rowena MacFarlane had always acted impetuously, allowed her heart to rule her head.

'Mark my words, lass, that habit of taking to people straight away will land you in trouble one day,' her mother had warned her. 'You should hold folk at bay for a wee while, just till you can size them up.'

But no, with Rowena it was in for a penny in for a pound, right from the start.

Besides, she did not feel that having a baby was a problem. To her, a baby was a gift, a joy. Her own people would be equally accepting of this wonderful, new addition...

Unfortunately, Lizzie Campbell, her mistress, had not been brought up by Romanies.

As far as Lizzie was concerned, Rowena's baby was a shame and a disgrace – not just to the slut of a mother but to all the good-living, law-abiding, hard-working folk on the farm.

Poor wee lambie, Rowena mused. How

could a sweet, innocent baby ever be a disgrace?

And so she had waited for her own folk and she had been there when wee Colin Campbell had come running back from the river with his excited account of wood fires and pretty wagons and a powerful-looking man with an earring.

Marek...

Rowena had seen him as soon as she'd approached the camp. How could you not see him? He was so tall, so dark, so intensely masculine in a way that no other man was, except perhaps Da. But then Marek and Rowena's father shared the same blood.

'Welcome, Cousin!' Marek had greeted her warmly enough and she couldn't help but notice that Pheemie Stewart had flounced away from the fire, obviously put out.

Poor Pheemie. Would she never learn that the only way to attract a man was to pretend that you had no interest in him?

'Mam, bring us some ale,' he had demanded imperiously. No-one had minded his high-handedness. That was their way...

When they'd been seated comfortably around the fire, like in the old times, they had spoken in their native tongue, the language that seems so foreign to non-Romanies. Some said they'd learned it first in Galway, others in Spain.

61

'I'd like to travel with you again, Marek.'

He had glanced pointedly at the gentle swelling in her abdomen. 'I take it he no longer wants you, then?'

'He *never* wanted me. Moon madness. I suppose – or maybe too much ale.'

'And you?'

'Ach, maybe I went a bit mad for a minute, too! The bairn's father is a good man, Marek. It's a real shame. This situation is destroying him and putting a lot of pressure on his marriage.

'Mind you, maybe that's no bad thing. What a mealy-mouthed woman he chose to be mistress of his farm.'

'I heard the farm was hers – handed down from her father...'

'Well, that would explain a few things, but he's in thrall to her. He likes her to be ladylike, to sew useless bits of pretty flowers and suchlike.

'They haven't learned that even beautiful things should be practical. Their ways are not ours. Maybe Lizzie Campbell should see your mother's wagon.'

'Well, her boy wanted to, right enough. It would have done the lad no harm, but thankfully Pheemie reminded me about the warped minds these folk have. They'd probably have raised a hullaballoo.'

He leaned forward to stir the fire's ashes with a stick and the resultant red glow painted his cheeks. 'When do you want to come?'

'As soon as I've said goodbye to the bairns.'

'Fair enough. You can live with my mother and she'll attend you when your time comes. Then we'll talk again, Rowena MacFarlane.'

She looked up at him through her long, dark lashes, so like his own. 'Talk? Aren't you and Pheemie Stewart doing all the "talking" that's needed?'

He shrugged. 'She lacks your fire, Rowena. You shouldn't have stormed out like that. I'd forgotten how easy it is to upset a proud woman like you.

'Let's get to know one another again while we wait for the little one and then, who knows...? I've missed you.'

'That's just because there's no-one here to answer you back! It's all – "yes, Marek. How clever you are, Marek"!'

He laughed. 'And isn't that the way it should be? 'Twould be different if I were a poor leader, but you have to admit that my father's mantle hangs well on my shoulders.'

'Ay, and his conceit an' all!'

He laughed as she stood up and took her hands. He was so tall and strong that she was forced to stand still.

'You always knew me better than anybody, Rowena. I meant it, you know – I really have missed you,' he said again and his voice was as dark as his hair.

'Have you not missed me?'

Rowena looked up at him through the incredible fringe of her lashes and smiled.

'Ay. It felt like a cured toothache. I knew something niggling was gone but I wasn't sure what it was!'

And she walked away from him as proudly as ever.

Looking after her, he laughed his deep, low laugh. She was coming back to him and what had happened to her between leaving and returning was of no importance.

The Watchnight Service was well under way. The asthmatic old organ had fought and eventually won the battle to fill the church with music.

There was no choir. They were not grand enough for a choir here, but there were good voices aplenty in the congregation and the joyous strains of Christmas carols soared into the rafters, swirled around with the smoke from the candles and settled, at last, on the holly boughs culled from Angus Campbell's own bushes.

He, however, saw nothing.

She'll not go!

Angus sat on a hard bench in the church at the dawning of Christmas Day and made the silent vow to himself.

He did not know how he would keep it but he knew that he could not let Rowena MacFarlane go. More importantly, he could not let his unborn child go. His over-active brain toyed with various ideas.

Rowena was a gypsy. The baby probably meant nothing to her. She would give it up – probably be glad to be shot of it. Yes, that was it!

He would confess everything to Lizzie, beg her for forgiveness and then live a life of remorse, and amendment.

He would be the best husband, the best father, the best farmer in the world, and, in return, Lizzie would forgive him for his moment of weakness and take Rowena's baby into her house.

He could not expect her to love the infant as she loved her own – the world, alas, is not a perfect place – but she would give the child, *his* child, a home.

Angus decided he would talk to the minister immediately after the service. He knew that a smoother tongue than his would be needed to win Lizzie over.

Never had a service seemed to take so long. He was even more feverish with expectation than the few children who had been allowed to stay awake.

They longed for the service to end, because, thanks to the old Queen and her late Consort, at home there was a

Christmas tree with wax candles waiting to be lit under the tree; who knows, maybe even a brown paper parcel from a mysterious figure called Santa Claus...

At last, the service was over, the church was empty and Angus and the Reverend Walter Grey stood together in the tiny vestry, the festive collection in wooden plates on the table in front of them.

'You'll be wanting to get home, Reverend.'

He was counting the collection, a great pile of farthings, halfpennies, pennies and, here and there, a crown – and at least one whole guinea.

'Indeed, Angus. You, too, presumably...'

'Well, I don't want to keep you from your bed.'

The minister looked at Angus, a man whose honesty and straightforwardness had always impressed him. Now, though, the farmer looked careworn and anxious.

'Angus, if you've got problems, I'm in no hurry. I'm here to help if I can.' The minister brushed his gown and hung it carefully on the peg at the back of the door while he thought of what he should say.

'You've seemed distracted recently. I've thought once or twice that you might have more than the price of grain on your mind.'

'Ay, I need to talk to someone.'

Angus looked around the cold vestry. There were still a few candles sending some tiny rays of light on to the coins, but he was very aware of the penetrating cold.

The Reverend Grey was not a young man.

'Look, Minister, I'll call round to the Manse in a day or so, when your family's out. That'd be better, I think.'

The minister fumbled with cold fingers at a drawer in the old chest beside him and took out a small bottle. He held it up to the light.

'This has been here for eleven Christ-mases now and there's still a drop left in it. Communion cups of brandy will hardly make us tipsy, Angus, but they'll definitely stay the cold. Here, drink it down.'

He handed the farmer a cut-glass goblet.

Angus gasped as the fiery liquid burned its way down his throat but it did give him courage of a sort.

'The thing is, I've – I've done something terrible, Minister, and if it comes out, the shame won't be mine alone but also Lizzie's and the boys'.'

Walter Grey, who had heard every sad story imaginable several times before, waited patiently.

'My wife's maid servant – well, she's having a babby, Minister.' He could say no more but hung his head shamefully.

'And the girl's family?' the minister enquired.

'She has none as far as I know. She's a

gypsy. There are gypsies wintering near the river, I hear, and she's kin to some of them, I think. She'll go off with them soon.'

Walter Grey was a practical man. 'Well, then, your problem's solved! One more gypsy babe will hardly make tongues wag.'

Angus slammed the glass goblet down so hard that it broke. Then he cursed as the glass cut him when he clumsily attempted to tidy up.

'Angus, Angus, you're overwrought! Look, forget the glass – we've more of them than we need.'

'Minister, this is not a gypsy baby,' Angus explained. 'It's mine!'

The last vestiges of colour drained from Walter Grey's already-pale face and he sighed.

'I've done something terrible,' Angus had said. That was an understatement...

'Does Lizzie know?' the minister asked softly when he could speak calmly.

'Not that it's mine. If that ever comes out, everything's finished. Help me, Reverend. Please help me.'

'Can you not tell her, Angus, and beg for forgiveness? After all, you'll have to beg forgiveness from the lass – and from God.'

Angus shook his head. Tell Lizzie? No, he'd toyed with that idea, but had now decided against it. If he told her, his life would be all but over. Again, he became aware of how cold it was in the church. Lizzie would be at home and already in bed, warm and asleep.

'Things haven't been going well between us for a year or two. James following Colin so quickly, you know, and Lizzie not being very strong...'

Reverend Grey had known Lizzie Campbell for more years than the man in front of him and he had a fair idea of just how strong she was, but he said nothing.

An image of his own family came into his head. They'd all be at home on this Christmas morning – except for his erstwhile son.

'We all have our crosses to bear, Angus, and there's no getting away from the fact that you have sinned. Sinned, Angus, against the laws of matrimony – and of God.'

He fought down compassion for the previously-untarnished man beside him. But there was no excuse for Angus's shocking aberration; no excuse whatsoever.

'Pull yourself together, man! The girl will no doubt find herself a husband among the gypsy band. Your punishment for grievous sin – and that's what it is, Angus – is that your child will not know your face.

'But surely that's a small price to pay? Children bring sorrow as well as joy, you know,' he said more softly.

69

Angus fell to his knees at the minister's feet. 'I can't let my bairn go. I just can't! It might starve, be hurt … or worse…'

The minister looked down on the bowed head with distaste. 'You want it all, Angus Campbell. Well, you can't marry this unfortunate lass yourself, so you'll have to find her a man who will.

'Why don't you go to the market at Friockheim on Thursday – or there's the Muckle Market at Montrose on Saturday? There are always one or two men there looking for a job.'

'Marriage is no' exactly a job,' Angus muttered and, for the first time, was able to smile a little.

Walter Grey echoed his smile. 'Well, it is and it isn't! But maybe there'll be a decent man there who could be persuaded to take her on if the lass agrees.

'He'll get a fair bit out of the deal – a job, a wife, a tied cottage … and the first bairn a wee bit early. Still, it won't be the first time that's happened.'

The minister's proposition made sense, even though the last thing the farm needed was a new worker. In the winter, there was barely enough work for the men for whom Angus was already responsible.

But he was also deeply responsible for Rowena MacFarlane.

And for the bairn…

Angus Campbell found Rowena alone after dinner the next day, when Lizzie, pleading exhaustion from the boys' high spirits, had taken to her bed for an afternoon nap.

James was also asleep, tired out, his father thought, by running backwards and forwards to the door looking for the snow which still had not come, and wee Colin was in the barn playing with the cats...

'I don't want you to go, Rowena,' he told her simply.

She looked at him and he thought he saw faint contempt in her eyes.

'Maybe I have no rights – to the bairn, I mean – but I can't stand the idea of him living in a wagon or a tent, being hounded out of towns. He's my flesh and blood, Rowena, and I want him raised properly. I'm his father...'

She almost spat. 'I'll raise *my* bairn right!' she said.

'He has a right to part of this,' he said, waving his hand vaguely around the farm.

'You're awfu' sure it'll be a boy... Fair enough – you've got two others, I suppose. Right then, give his inheritance to me to keep for him. Give it to me now.'

'You know I can't do that. One day, though, I promise, he'll have a younger son's share, the same as James.' He stood up from his chair by the fire and went over to the door where she was standing, ready, it seemed, to run.

'Rowena, obviously I can't marry you, and I doubt you'd want me anyway, but try to understand my feelings. That night, well, I was mad.' He stopped and straightened as if gathering the remnants of his hurt pride.

'Mad with desire, I suppose, with longing. I couldn't help myself. You're so beautiful...

'But what I did, what *we* did, was wrong. I yielded to temptation, gave in to the weakness of the flesh. And now you're having my child and, as I said, I can't marry you.

'But other men would be glad, honoured, to have you as their wife.'

'Name them!' she said curtly, moving away from him.

He looked at her outline against the window and wondered that she did not seem to see what he saw, a magnificent, fruitful woman, in the full flush of her beauty.

'I'll name them tomorrow, after I've been to the feein' mart at Friockheim.'

She turned back, her eyes filled with contempt. 'So you're planning to find me a man, like you might find your cows a bull. No thanks! I'll find my own man, Maister – as I did before.'

He flushed at the disappointment and more, the humour, in her voice.

'Be sensible, Rowena, for the bairn's sake.'

She opened the door and the first flakes of snow blew in with the icy wind.

'Marek will send word soon, and I'll go. Meantime, you hang on to your damned inheritance, for *my* bairn won't need it.'

On those words, the door slammed behind her.

But somewhere deep within her the farmer's genuine concern had struck a chord.

Windmill Bar,
Dundee,
Christmas, 1895

'Strap me, what a feast! The only thing missing is a boar's head!'

The speaker was the only young man in the company not in the uniform of one of her Majesty's regiments.

'My dear Matt, you should have told us you wanted one. With money, old boy, *anything's* possible.'

Matthew Grey peered through the thick, tobacco smoke at his old school friend, Captain the Honourable Roderick Forsythe, and laughed. On this particular Christmas night, there was nothing

73

remotely honourable about dear old Roddy.

He'd drunk far too much claret, dallied with the good-time girls attracted to the glamour of the uniform and the charm of his cash – much of which he'd frittered away in ill-considered wagers.

Matthew, himself an inveterate gambler, pulled the dice from his pocket and tossed them on to the table. Ah, his luck had held – or had it? Yes! Three sixes!

'Pass me the red biddy, Roddy,' he said, chuckling with relief. 'For a moment there, I thought I'd had it.

'Could have lost the lot again and been forced to go on the wagon, old son. Nightmare!'

Roddy laughed lazily and reached across the buxom girl on his lap for a wine bottle. Pouring some out for his friend, then kissing the girl passionately, he finally asked, 'Do you rise and go to bed on the roll of a dice, Matt?'

'Pretty well,' Matt said in all seriousness. 'Saves thinking, dear boy.' He laughed again. 'So what do you think of my Christmas spread?'

Roderick surveyed the scene through reddened, cigar-smoke-stung eyes. A long, oak dining-table was piled with the remains of a sumptuous banquet.

Holly and ivy garlands decorated the table and the necks of several of his fellow officers and their scantily-clad paramours.

Where once there had been order, there was now a confusion of half-eaten food, overflowing wine glasses and ale tankards, and glittering candles.

'Not bad, old son. Must have cost a bomb,' he said, his voice slurred.

'Right – order up some hot punch, old man. We brave lads will soon have to be on our way. Regiment ships out next week.

'You should come with us, Matt. Three weeks of non-stop fun followed by three months of hard slog! It's the only way to live. Come and join us!'

His fellow officers and the girls cheered wildly at this sentiment but Matt did not share their enthusiasm. The army... He was not rich like Roderick. Was he clever enough, strong enough, to rise through the ranks on his own merits?

'No, I think I'll pass on that offer, Roddy. You need brains to cut the mustard as an officer. My sister got all of those in my family, I'm afraid.'

'Who needs brains?' Roddy countered. 'I can't remember having any! All you need is money, or an ability to do what you're told, Matthew.'

'There – I knew there was something stopping me!' Matt laughed and emptied his wine glass at a gulp.

Doing as he was told wasn't his strong

point. Damn it! Life would be so easy if he did not love his family so much.

He saw his father, worn out by the demands of his parish, yet happy in his work. His mother struggling to make ends meet, still wearing the hat she had worn every winter Sunday for at least ten years.

Did the Reverend Grey guess that she had sent ten whole shillings to her son?

Matt looked at the grooming table, which held the carcass of a goose, a turkey, several capons and a sirloin of beef.

None of these fine meats would have graced the Manse table – yet that ten bob of his father's hard-earned money had, with the turn of a dice, paid for this bacchanalian feast and for the suit of clothes he wore.

Le mot juste – the last word – in Victorian elegance! He turned abruptly and tossed another log on the fire.

As he did so, Matt caught sight of himself in the gilt-framed mirror above the fireplace.

The man before him was tall and slender with blond hair and brilliant blue eyes shaded by long eyelashes that any girl would envy.

For all that, Matthew was the epitome of masculinity. He had that *'je ne sais quoi'* that no woman could resist. Eventually every woman succumbed to his charms – only to be discarded at his whim.

Every woman but his sister, of course – Sarah, the dedicated school ma'am. She had a fine, academic brain that had earned her, with comparative ease, a splendid degree.

For all that, she would never land the position of Dominie – head teacher – because she was, after all, only a woman.

Poor Sarah who yearned for a husband and children and knew that to have them would mean sacrificing her other love, teaching.

She had asked him to go home to their parents' house for the festive season.

'You owe it to them, Matt.'

'Oh, Sarah, "owe" is such an unkind word. I owe them nothing, having asked for nothing.'

Sarah had turned away from him, poor Sarah who had been blessed with the brains instead of the looks.

'I went shopping in Dundee with Mamma only last Saturday,' she said quietly. 'We were supposed to be buying her a new bonnet. I suppose you didn't ask for the ten shillings she had saved.'

'Of course I didn't!'

'Oh, grow up, Matt!' she had railed. 'Where do you think she got that kind of money? She scrimped and saved and did without! And you'll only gamble it away...'

But he had not gambled it away. He had won and won and won and there were the remains of his festive feast to prove it, and this fine evening suit, and solid silver cufflinks to rival Roddy Forsythe's.

He would take them to the pawn shop as soon as he was sober and Mamma, his dear, dear mother would have her new hat after all.

But that was enough forward planning. There was still tonight to enjoy...

'Landlord, hot punch for my guests,' he called. 'We can't let them brave the rigours of a cold Dundee winter without due fortification...'

At last the snow had come and gladdened the hearts of the children at least.

'You know where to find us if you change your mind, Rowena.'

'I won't, Marek.'

'You're being stupid staying behind – you must see that. One last chance, come with us...'

Rowena shook her head and stepped back from him and Marek climbed up to the front of his wagon. He picked up the reins in his strong, brown fingers and urged the muscular horse forward.

Without looking back again, he led the caravan of wagons along the river and back on to the road.

They would travel west, find a drier site nearer a town where there was at least the chance of some occasional work.

Rowena watched until they were out of sight, her feelings mixed. But Angus Campbell's words had moved her. In all conscience, she could not deprive him of his own flesh and blood...

I must be mad, she said to herself. But, first and foremost, the baby is mine. I can care for him myself – but his father would help if times got really hard.

She stood, wrapped in her old tweed shawl, as the snow blew thicker and thicker around her and watched until the wagons were no longer visible. Marek's was red and gold, his mother's yellow, Pheemie's was green and yet now, no colour seemed to stand out.

Everything was a dull grey, the earth, the sky, the disappearing wagons ... her spirit.

But the voice that haunted her dreams came to her again as she stood in the cold watching her 'last chance' disappear around a bend in the river.

Despite everything, she still had feelings for Angus. He was a fine man – and this unborn child obviously meant a great deal to him.

'Maybe I have no rights, but I can't stand the idea of him living in a wagon, being hounded out of town.'

'Well then, Angus Campbell,' she said, as she turned back towards the house, 'this way, you may watch the child grow, but much good will it do you.'

She brushed moisture from her eyes. She could not call it tears.

Rowena MacFarlane, last of a proud line, would not weep. Somehow she would survive – and if she desperately needed help with her child, its father would be there … but only as a last resort.

Now the snow that had threatened for days was making up for all its promises.

The steady fall had become a raging blizzard and Rowena began to panic. She could hardly see her hand before her face...

The road to the farm went … that way, wasn't it? Surely the hedge, where the wild brambles grew in the autumn, was there just on her left? No, shouldn't the hedge be on her right approaching the house…?

Think, Rowena, think.

She stayed calm. It's my condition, she told herself. That must be why I'm so confused.

Think! Come on … *think!*

She could no longer see the river nor could she hear it. Indeed, she could hear nothing but the thudding of her heart.

Go on, Rowena. Even if you're going the wrong way, you'll come to the river eventually, she reasoned. *Once you do, you'll find your bearings again. See, it's simple.*

But her shawl was so wet that its weight was a real burden now and it was becoming more and more difficult to see.

You're not far from the farmhouse, Rowena, she encouraged herself. Of course the mistress wants you gone, but for all that, she's a woman and a mother – she'll not leave you to die in the snow. Just keep going … keep going…

She took off her shawl to shake the weight of the snow from it and the driving wind caught it and whipped it from her hands into the impenetrable white-out.

She stumbled blindly after it, cursing herself for her weakness and her folly.

And now she was completely lost and frozen to the marrow. The wind seemed to drive the snow from all directions. Where was the farm? Where was the river?

Exhausted, Rowena sank down for a moment to rest. The snow would blow over soon, surely? A few minutes more and these icy winds would tire of their games.

But they did not…

Matt Grey, nursing a throbbing hangover and a mouth that was as dry as a sandpit, had been dropped off at the end of the main road by a congenial carter.

The snow started when he was less than halfway to the village and he cursed his stupidity in squandering his winnings on evening dress instead of a warm, woollen overcoat.

'And these useless, ruddy shoes!'

What had possessed him to journey from the fine hotels of Edinburgh to the wilds of Forfarshire in evening pumps?

Still, everything rests on the turn of the cards, he mused philosophically. And the cards eventually took my fair-weather friends and every last farthing of my winnings from me.

Never mind, there's always a welcome to be had at home ... even if it is faintly disapproving at times.

That morning, after he had settled his hotel bill – unlike the Honourable Roderick, who somehow never paid for anything – he had cut the cards and they had decreed that he should go home, tail between his legs, and do whatever his father told him to.

Maybe he'll suggest schoolmastering like Sarah, he thought. He suddenly shuddered and it wasn't the snow that made him do it.

Or that I should follow him into the ministry...

In spite of the cold, he laughed. If his father had ever nurtured such hopes, they were long gone.

At first, Matthew didn't notice the bundle lying in the snow. When he did eventually see it, he ignored it. Some careless carter had obviously lost, or dumped, a bundle of rags.

But then the rags moaned and stirred

slightly and, curious, Matt turned and went back to investigate.

The 'rags' turned out to be a woman. Her condition was poor. Indeed, Matt reckoned she was almost dead. Yet she was young, judging by the darkness of the eyelashes that fanned across her white face.

He lifted her up. She was surprisingly heavy and, as she stirred weakly in his arms, he saw her condition.

'Dear God, fancy being thrown out by her lover on a night like this.' He spoke the words out loud.

'I've no coat to give you, lass,' he said compassionately, 'but I'll do my damnedest to get you back to my parents' house.'

The girl's eyes opened and they looked at one another. Lively, brilliant blue eyes smiled into deep, dark pools. 'I just pray that my mother believes me when I tell her I'm not responsible for your condition,' he muttered to her as he shifted his grip.

'Please,' she whispered faintly and he heard her teeth chattering.

She was in a really bad way. Whoever had thrown her out had no doubt hoped that the cruel weather would solve his problem – and it looked as if he may yet be right.

The girl was completely exhausted, and what's more, had almost given up the struggle for survival.

'Come on, lass,' Matt urged. 'Nothing's as

bad as it seems. I'll take you home to my mother. A plate of her tattie broth could melt an iceberg! And my sister'll be there. She'll have some good, dry clothes you can wear.'

More than once during their struggle to the Manse, he thought they would not make it. His own clothes were totally unsuited to the weather. He was tired and wet and cold and the girl was a dead weight in his arms.

But he could not leave her.

'The cards didn't warn me about you, Miss … Miss… What is your name?'

He bent to catch the faint word.

'Rowena.'

'How romantic,' he told her. *And how pagan,* he added to himself.

Despite the desperate situation they were in, he laughed ruefully when he pictured himself introducing his unexpected guest to his father.

'Leave me,' she whispered then. 'Save yourself.'

'And lose my chance of being a hero! Rowena, my dear Rowena, you'll be the saving of me. We'll save one another.

'There, see that light ahead? It's the Manse, my – my parents' home. We've made it, lass! Lady Luck had smiled on us!'

It was his father who came to the door and who took the sodden woman from his arms.

'Happy Christmas, Father,' Matthew said wearily to the astonished Reverend Grey. 'I've brought you a surprise present.'

Matt Grey recognised the subtle difference in the tones of the voices at the Manse. His mother, his sister, and Elsie, their maid-of-all-work, had rushed to the door when he and his cold, wet, exhausted companion had staggered up the driveway and on to the porch.

At first it had been himself who had captured all their attention. Matthew, the son of the house, a sore trial at times perhaps, but still the son of the house and a gentleman...

'Dear Matt!' they'd clucked. 'Poor Matt. You're soaked through. Come in, or you'll catch your death.'

And there had been equally solicitous cluckings over the exhausted Rowena.

Then what instinct was it that quickly told such women that this girl was not of their class? That she was not quite so worthy of their loving care?

Oh, they would do their Christian duty. The voices were sympathetic as they trotted out appropriate phrases...

'In your condition ... such dreadful

weather … can't think why your employer…'

But now Matt heard that the voices held no real warmth. That was all directed at the prodigal son.

'Right, straight to bed with you and I'll bring up a bowl of my best soup, Matt.' That was Elsie, who had worked for Matthew's parents every day for, as far as he knew, 40 years.

'There's still a nightshirt of yours in the tallboy, Matt,' his mother added. 'Where's your luggage by the way? Och, it doesn't matter – I'm sure it'll be sent on soon.'

He was too tired to tell her there was no luggage. He was too weary to admit to her that he had squandered her money on a fabulous Christmas feast and that what he'd had left had disappeared with his erstwhile friends while he'd slept off his debauchery.

Now, though, Rowena was quiet, *too* quiet.

'Mother, please take care of that poor girl. She's in a really bad way.

'It was incredible finding her abandoned like that. I still can't believe it, but someone must have thrown her out in that awful weather.'

Still Rowena, her lustrous black eyelashes so dark against her pale cheeks, kept her eyes closed.

Chrissie Grey looked at the girl and sniffed. This added burden was the last thing she needed.

She knew this was the gypsy girl who worked for the Campbells. She was obviously expecting, so all the rumours were true.

But why her Walter should have to cope with the Campbells' unwanted problems Chrissie did not know.

'We'd best get you out of those wet things, my lass, and into a warm bed. My maid can lend you a nightie.'

At that, Rowena's dark eyes flew open and she glared at Mrs Grey so disdainfully that the older woman coloured furiously. How dare the trollop!

Rowena's haughty look said that she was well aware that of the three women in the kitchen, it was the minister's wife who was closest to her in size.

'No-one threw me out, Mistress,' Rowena said softly. 'And the weather, like so much else, is God's will.'

Chrissie Grey gasped and it was her daughter, Sarah, who took charge of their unwelcome guest.

'Come along then,' she said firmly, as she almost manhandled Rowena from the room and up the uncarpeted wooden staircase.

'You can argue about God's will and the free will He gave each of us with me if you want! But I warn you now, I'm used to these arguments.

'Anyway, I think my brother has saved your life and, no doubt you'll be grateful to him when you're dry and rested. The upstairs rooms are cold, I'm afraid.

'This is a Manse and there's never enough coal to go round, but I'll bring you a hot-water pig for your feet and some of Elsie's soup for nourishment.

'You'll have to forgive her for fussing over Matt so much. It's just that she helped bring him up and he's special to her.'

'Maybe your brother should just have left me to die in the snow,' Rowena remarked, her voice filled with the despair of exhaustion.

Sarah laughed. 'Oh, what melodrama! You must be feeling better. You're beginning to sound sorry for yourself! The thing is, if no-one threw you out, what were you doing out on the road in your condition?'

The smile faded and Sarah pulled herself up. She had gone too far.

'Listen, don't answer that. It's none of my business. The point is you're here and you need help.'

Deftly, Sarah had been stripping off Rowena's wet clothes.

'You poor thing,' she said softly as the gypsy girl stood before her trying to stop shivering. 'Come on, into bed with you!

'I'm sorry – I should have brought you a nightgown first. I'm fine with schoolchildren, but I've no experience with adults, I'm afraid.

'The bed's cold but not damp and the bottle will warm you up in no time. That and some home-baked bread with the soup, eh? Would you like that?'

Sarah looked down at Rowena, so pale on the white pillows, and genuine pity and perplexity stirred within her.

No man, as far as she knew, had ever desired Sarah. Yet this mere tinker lass was – she searched for an appropriate euphemism and found one – in the family way, and even Matt, sophisticated, elegant Matt, had almost killed himself trying to save her.

What was this magical quality that some women had and some lacked? Ah well, she had quite resigned herself to being without it.

At least she would never be found in a ditch in a snowstorm.

'I'll get you the soup,' she said softly and when Rowena made no answer, she added, 'Accept it for your baby's sake. The child's the reason you let Matt pull you out of the ditch, isn't it?'

Left alone, Rowena shivered against the icy folds of starched linen and hoped that the daughter of the Manse would remember the nightgown.

I had no choice but to let him help me, she mused. Funnily enough, I wasn't thinking of

89

the baby, more of Marek and Angus and of the rights and wrongs of letting my people leave without me.

These folk in this Manse have made their disapproval very clear. Cold as charity, they say.

Well, this bed certainly is, but Matt? He's very different, is Matt...

The delicious smell of baking bread awakened Rowena next morning and she lay disorientated for a moment thinking that she was a child again in her mother's wagon.

But then her own baby stirred in her womb and she remembered exactly where she was and opened her eyes and looked around.

A weak winter sun was trying to warm the room, dancing across the rag rug and lighting up the sprigs of forget-me-nots on the wallpaper.

A very dark and unhappy painting entitled *The Good Shepherd* stared down at her from the opposite wall and Rowena decided, correctly, that the artist had never seen a shepherd or a sheep.

She lay for a minute enjoying the warmth of the bed, the peace of the room, the smell of bread that she had not baked, and then the door opened.

Mrs Chrissie Grey came bustling in with a tray.

'You're awake then,' she said brusquely. 'I looked in on you before I went to bed last night and all seemed well.'

'Yes, I'm fine, thank you, Mistress.' Rowena had not expected such solicitude.

She looked down quickly and discovered she was wearing a nightgown. Of course, the daughter had brought it to her with the hot-water vessel, now stone cold, and the soup, long eaten.

Now there was a bowl of porridge on the tray, a toasted muffin and a mug of tea. It looked and smelled wonderful.

'Eat up, Rowena, and then we'll discuss what we're going to do with you.'

There was no warmth in the face that looked down at her and, despite the comfort of the bed, Rowena felt cold.

She was definitely not welcome here. Was she welcome anywhere? With her own people, of course, but she had sent them away.

'I'm feeling a lot better. I won't cause you any more trouble, Mistress. Thank you for...'

Chrissie dumped the tray on Rowena's lap. 'Do you know whose house you're in, girl? My husband, the minister, now feels responsible for you.

'If the road's clear, he'll go over to the Campbells and tell them you're here.'

Rowena almost knocked over the tea in

91

her agitation. 'No, please, there's no need. I'd meant to speak to Mr Campbell myself.'

Chrissie was shocked by such boldness. She meant to speak to the *master* and her employed by the mistress.

'You'd do better to speak to whichever of his men is responsible for your condition!' she said tartly before she could control her anger.

'Marriage is the answer. Responsibility, I've never shirked my duty and this man must be made to do his by you.

'It's hardly the best start for Holy Matrimony, but one must accept that you're not the first and no doubt will not be the last girl to fall into sin.

'Now eat your breakfast and I'll see what I can find for you to wear. Your dress and petticoats are still on the pulley in the kitchen. They're too damp to put on this morning.

'Elsie will lend you something respectable. I see Sarah gave you one of her own nightgowns. I embroidered that myself, you know.'

Rowena's hand went to the fine crochet at the neck of the warm lawn. She had never worn such expensive material before.

'It's lovely,' she said. 'It was very good of Miss Sarah. I thank her, too, for her kindness.'

'My daughter knows her Christian duty.'

Mrs Grey went to the washstand by the window and picked up the jug that sat in the basin. 'I'll send up some water.

'Sarah told me how clean you were–' she sounded surprised '–and I'm sure Mrs Campbell will be pleased that you've not disgraced her.'

She opened the door to go out and Matt's angry voice came to them.

'Good grief, Father, exactly how much grovelling do you expect me to do?'

And the minister answered in a voice that was just as hurt, just as angry.

'As much as it takes! You and that tinker you brought into your mother's house are a well-matched pair, are you not? She's a hussy and you're a complete waster!

'Your university career came to nothing – despite the sacrifices we made to put you there!

'No, I've had enough, Matthew. Christmas or no Christmas, you'll get out there and you'll find a job and you'll keep it!'

Chrissie stood stock still. Rowena looked at her rigid back and imagined the look of grief that must be on the mother's face. So it was not only the poor who had their problems.

Matt, her saviour, her strong support in the storm, was, it seemed, a wastrel and his genuine act of kindness had simply landed him in more trouble.

'I'll dress and go, Mistress,' she said quietly to Mrs Grey, who seemed unable to either go or return. 'I don't want to be any bother...'

'You'll do no such thing! I know my duty, Miss!' Mrs Grey almost hissed. 'Mr Grey will tell the Campbells that you're here.

'If they won't take you in and deal with the problem, my husband will take you to the workhouse. At least there you'll have a roof over your head until the child is born.'

She closed the door quietly and Rowena, appetite gone, lay back against the pillows while the word *workhouse* chased itself around and around in her head.

Lizzie Campbell was thrilled to have a visit from someone as important as the minister.

'Come in, Mr Grey, come in. Although it's not quite the New Year yet, I almost feel as though you're my first foot.

'Angus is down at the bothy this very minute discussing the requirements for the Hogmanay party.'

She led the way into the parlour, the best room, chatting, chatting all the way.

'May was the last celebration here – after the Feein' Market, you know. We've just been so busy. Here, let me take your coat and I'll send wee Colin down to fetch his father.

'Now would you like some tea, or something a wee bit stronger?'

Walter Grey declined both. He did not want to discuss Rowena MacFarlane with Lizzie Campbell. He was sure that Angus had not told his wife about his own part in the maid's downfall, and, therefore, Walter had decided that it was not his place to tell the sordid tale to the wronged wife.

He managed to assure Lizzie that Springhill Farm would be one of his first ports of call in 1896.

'If all the bustle back at the Manse is anything to go by, Lizzie, you good ladies must have more than enough to do at the moment.

'When I do come, however, I'll expect some of your excellent shortbread with my cup of tea.

'In the meantime, my business with Angus will take no time at all.'

He regretted his words as soon as he stepped out into the farmyard, where muck and snow had been churned together into a ghastly sort of sludgy porridge by the hooves of horses and cattle.

Walter was wearing his galoshes, which were splendid for the journey up the pebbled road to the kirk, but uncomfortably inadequate for a farm track.

Icy mud oozed over the tops of his footwear and in no time at all his socks and, of course, his poor feet were wet and cold.

Suddenly, in his mind's eye, he saw his son on the doorstep, wearing only light evening shoes and carrying the exhausted figure of Rowena MacFarlane.

Both of us with frozen feet, Walter mused – the son for one reason, the father for another.

And which of us is the better Christian?

Angus Campbell was seated at a table near a roaring fire. Tam Laird was with him and two of the orramen. They were drinking strong, hot tea from mugs the cleanliness of which would not bear scrutiny.

'Minister,' Angus exclaimed, 'what a surprise to see you here! Come away in.' The invitation was warm enough, but Walter recognised a note of fear in the merry voice. 'We're planning a Ne'erday celebration to put all others to shame.'

'Well, remember it's a pagan festival, Angus, and that control and moderation should be exercised as well as drinking arms!'

'Indeed, indeed. It's just the old customs, Minister – you know, tradition…'

The two lads had pulled up the best chair for the minister and he was forced to sit before a blazing fire that sent out almost unbearable heat.

'Well, you certainly keep yourselves comfortable here, lads. I trust you'll not leave a fire like this unguarded.'

'Och, no, Minister. Did you no' see in the paper that a whole steading went up afore Christmas when some daft loon lit a fire to warm the bothy and then went into the toon to the dancing?

'No, we're no' that daft here at Springhill.'

'I'm glad to hear it.' Walter smiled as he tried to edge his chair away from the fierce heat. How could they not notice it? He would never complain about the cold in the Manse again.

The men eventually left to attend to their work and Angus and Walter were left alone.

Angus was ill at ease. This was an unexpected, extraordinary visit. Parish business would have been conducted openly under Lizzie's watchful eyes and with a loaded tea tray between them. What was all this about?

Walter quickly put him out of his agony.

'Rowena MacFarlane's at the Manse, Angus. My son–' he did not realise how bleak his features became as he said the words '–my son found her in a ditch yesterday, half dead in that snowstorm. He brought her home to his mother.'

'But she went off with the gypsies, didn't she?' Angus had prayed that she would not go, but now he could not believe that she was still here, and in trouble. 'Merciful heavens, Minister. That's terrible! Is she well?'

'She's a tinker, Angus. It's not the first time she'd been out in a storm. She's a survivor.

'All of which means your little, er, problem still hasn't been solved. So what are you going to do about her?'

Angus sprang up from his seat and it was not the fierce heat from the fire that drove him to walk nervously about the bothy.

'As God's my judge, I don't know what to do. Sometimes I wish I'd never gone to the damned Feein' Market.

'Tam Laird wouldn't be here right enough, but neither would Rowena Mac-Farlane and all the trouble that's come with her.'

'That's useless talk, Angus, empty words. I've thought long and hard and have decided that you're both at fault. You *knew* you were married and so did she!

'I hope all this has shown you how evil strong drink can be.

'Now, though, I take it you won't confess everything to Lizzie? No – well then, until the woman has birthed the child, the only place for her is the workhouse in Dundee.'

Angus looked at the minister while the shameful word, workhouse, hammered in his brain. Workhouse! Workhouse! Workhouse! His child, born in a workhouse?

It was an unbearable prospect but what else could he do? Could he find a husband for the girl? No – he'd tried that.

Nor could he afford, as wealthy men did, to set Rowena up somewhere with an adequate income.

Besides, he did not love her. To him, she was living proof of his weakness and he preferred not to see her but the child was quite different.

A child was more than an accident. This was *his* child, his son, just as Colin and James were his sons, and deserved the same decent standard of living.

But he could *not* tell Lizzie. She and her family would stick together resolutely and he would lose his wife, his children, and his farm – all for a moment's madness.

'Fair enough – take the lass to the workhouse, Reverend,' he said, feeling the shame corroding him. 'I'll do what I can for her and the bairn.'

Dressed in Elsie, the Greys' housekeeper's second-best dress of charcoal bombazine, Rowena stood in what Mrs Grey grandly called the library and tried not to think. Or was she thinking too hard?

The problem was of her own making and she had foolishly thrown away the decent solution Marek had offered…

She did not want the minister to appeal to the Campbells. All she'd wanted was to approach the father of her child for a little financial help just until the baby was born.

Now, because of that sudden blizzard, she was thrown on the mercy of the minister, who felt it was his Christian duty to deal with her.

She had tried to persuade them to give her her clothes and let her go. She could easily walk to Dundee: it was only about a 15-mile walk and a fair road all the way.

'You just sit there in the library until the Reverend gets back,' Elsie had instructed her as she had fussed around trying to make the dress fit better.

And the maid had refused all offers of help with the work in the house or the kitchen.

'No, I've got my own routine and I like to stick to it. The Mistress and Miss Sarah help a little now and again, as ladies should.'

I'll read a book then, Rowena thought.

Her mother had told her that her ability to read and write would be invaluable assets, but so far they had brought her nothing. She could read, but there were never any books.

In the Campbells' home, for example, there had been a bible, a tome on medical care, and a few uninspired children's books.

But here ... Rowena looked around the cold room and her spirits soared. Books, books, and more books.

'I hope they're not all holy books,' she said aloud and was startled when a low, humorous voice answered.

'No indeed they're not. Quite a lot of them are either mine or my sister's and she's addicted to romantic novels. Rubbish, my father calls them, but having paid for them, he's unwilling to consign them to the fire.

'Mind you, one winter, when we're low on coal, who knows? So grab your chance. Read now, Rowena MacFarlane – if you can.'

Matthew Grey, looking more like a farm worker than a gentleman of leisure, was sitting in an armchair beside a very frugal fire. Still incredibly good looking, he was reading ... Shelley.

Rowena had heard of Shelley. He was a poet.

Rowena simply laughed at Matt's half doubt about her literacy, showing her even white teeth.

He was stunned by her. His heart caught in his throat at the merry sound and at her incredible beauty, which, if anything, was enhanced by the bloom of pregnancy.

'Of course I can read,' she said. 'I'm part Irish. Women in Ireland were reading and writing with the monks when women in Scotland were still wearing animal skins!'

He was taken aback by that, but said nothing as she strolled along the shelves of books.

'Scott, Stevenson? Hardly trashy romantic novels, Mr Grey.'

'Oh, no doubt one day some erudite professor will decide that they're literature. Maybe they are, but if a girl gets her man at the end of a story is that not a romance, Miss MacFarlane?'

She smiled. 'Oh, sir, I couldn't begin to argue with an educated gentleman like yourself.' Then she added, 'But I did say they weren't *trashy* romances.'

At last, at last, Matt thought, a conversation with a female that was cut and thrust, rather than simper simper!

What a woman this Rowena MacFarlane was! With a woman like her beside him, a man could forget about cards and drink.

'You're bound for the workhouse, I hear, Rowena,' he said bluntly and felt sad as he saw her flinch.

'I'll survive,' she said quietly, almost as if she were trying to convince herself.

He watched her, looking more anxious since he'd mentioned the workhouse perhaps, as she walked along taking a book out here and there and looking at the pages for a moment before returning it to the shelf.

'Choose a few, Rowena.' He had not meant to upset her, yet he obviously had. 'Choose some now and take them with you and I'll come and bring you more later.'

She looked at him out of those great, dark eyes that had seen so much of sorrow and of joy and he felt that he was drowning.

'Would you really do that?' she asked gently. Instinctively, she knew he would if he said so. He *was* different, Matt Grey.

Was he a gentleman? Was that what a man who spoke to everybody as equals and treated everyone with kindness was?

'Of course I'd do it, Rowena,' he said, thrusting his father's opinions from his mind. 'Books will help you through the waiting.'

He looked at her and felt again her amazing strength coupled with fragility.

Extraordinary creatures, women, he thought, but this time he thought it humbly. 'The baby?' he began. He who knew nothing whatsoever about babies. 'When is it...?'

'In the spring,' she answered correctly in reply to his unspoken question.

'Well then, let's look forward to the spring. *The year's pleasant king*,' he added but, obviously she did not know that poem and he thought fleetingly that it might be pleasant to teach Rowena MacFarlane the joys of literature...

Dinner was served at midday in the Manse's dining-room. It was a large, bare room, completely without warmth and the feeble fire that half-heartedly tried to deal with the high, rather dingy room, finally coughed despairingly and went out.

'We just can't get a decent blaze going in this fireplace, Walter,' Chrissie Grey complained. 'I've had that chimney scoured till I could almost bleach linen in there and still it won't draw!'

Walter smiled at her. Poor Chrissie. In 40 years of marriage, he doubted if she had complained even 10 times.

What a perfect wife she was for a minister, especially one in a small Forfarshire parish, where the Manse was as big as a smart London hotel. Mind you, size was the *only* thing it had in common with a hotel.

It was a house that had been built for a man with ten children and at least three servants, inexhaustible supplies of coal, or a preference for bathing in ice water.

Walter had two children, one servant, who was probably now more of a burden than a help, and no money at all in the coffers.

Fortunately, local farmers were generous with what they grew. He was never short of potatoes, turnips, or fruit in season.

The odd leg of mutton occasionally found its way to the Manse kitchen, eggs in the summer, and sometimes a haunch of venison, or a few fine, fresh trout.

Sometimes, though, he felt that he would give all these perks away for one warm room, where icy draughts didn't steal under doors and where a fire would burn brightly at the end of a long day.

'Och well, it took the chill off the room while it lasted, Chrissie,' Walter replied gently.

Elsie served the soup in silence and they ate in silence.

Rowena sat with her eyes downcast for fear of catching anyone else's gaze.

Because of that, she was completely unaware of the fact that Matt could scarcely tear his eyes away from her. He was captivated by this gorgeous, exotic, exciting woman.

He smiled at her, got no response and then decided to challenge his father, who was obviously unwilling to speak.

'I take it you saw Campbell then, Father?' Matt saw Rowena tense.

'So what did he have to say, sir?'

Rowena's spoon, full of thin broth, was suspended inches from her lips.

'About what, Matthew?' The minister's tone was cold.

'About Miss MacFarlane here. He certainly owes her something, does he not?'

He saw a swift, startled glance pass between Rowena and his father.

Surprise at his question? That was a strange response, was it not?

'Surely any responsible employer has a moral obligation to his employee, Father?' Matthew added then, his expression puzzled.

Again Rowena's soup seemed to hold untold fascination for her.

'Not once she has left his employment,' Walter replied.

The only sound in the room was Rowena's sigh, but was it a sigh of relief, or of sorrow?

Matt was puzzled. 'Father?'

'Miss MacFarlane's business is not yours, Matthew. You should be more concerned with finding gainful employment.'

'Well, if you asked Mr Campbell about Rowena, who, you say, has no claim on him, perhaps you also asked him about employment for me.'

'I'll answer that with a tract from the good book – *In the sweat of thy face shalt thou eat bread*. When might I ask did you last sweat, Matthew?'

Chrissie suddenly lifted her apron over her head and burst into loud tears.

Matt looked embarrassed, Walter perplexed, Sarah furious and Rowena sat as if she had been turned to stone.

Sarah went to her mother and eased the apron down.

'Mother, you know their arguing means nothing. Drink up your soup, dear. Poor Elsie will think you don't like it.'

Matt looked into his soup plate and made a noise halfway between a snort and a laugh.

'I'm sorry, Father! Tempted though I am,

I won't even give a rude answer to that question.

'And, Mother, if you cry, I'll simply presume that you'd be happier if I left again.'

'Oh, Matthew dear, just once it would be so pleasant if you and your father could discuss things sensibly,' she answered sadly.

Matt pushed his half-finished plate of soup away from him.

'Miss MacFarlane is, no doubt, shocked by my bad manners, but I'll ask you again, sir, if Campbell is going to help Rowena in any way whatsoever.'

Walter stood up so abruptly that his heavy silver watch chain caught the rim of the plate and capsized it.

For a few seconds, he stood quietly, trying to compose himself, while the women stared at him and Matt studiously ignored him.

Then at last he spoke and his words hung in the air like icicles on the roof of a house, ready to crash on the unwary.

'Get out, sir! Leave this table and this house and do not return until you've found a job.'

Matt went quite white but he stood up and faced his father. There was a devilish smile playing on his lips.

'*I cannot dig: to beg I am ashamed,*' he said at last. 'That's the New Testament, Rowena

– Luke's gospel. Have you read it?'

'The labourer is worthy of his hire,' Rowena replied before she could stop herself and again Matt exulted at her wit.

'Poor Rowena,' he said. 'You're far too much of a woman for the yokel who'll get you.' He patted his sobbing mother and bent down to kiss her.

'Don't worry, I'll be back, dear. Doesn't the Prodigal son always return? I'll come back when I've found something worthy of my talents.'

'Oh, Matt, you've thrown away all your talents!' Sarah exclaimed sadly. 'Father, you can't mean to forbid him the house. He's your son, for goodness' sake!'

Walter was shaking with anger. His voice when he spoke was deep and un-compromising. 'I have no son.'

The only sound in the room was that of Chrissie's broken-hearted sobbing. Then Matt, looking tense, countered with, 'And I have no father!'

He turned to Rowena. 'You know, I've just remembered one of the best bits of Father's – the Reverend's – favourite book. *It is better to marry than to burn.'*

'Sarah, my dear, have mercy on all the little boys in your school: sometimes their parents are a wee bit to blame for their errant ways.'

'Get out, sir!' Walter almost shrieked and

Matt left quietly, closing the door softly behind him.

Walter sat down and rang the bell for Elsie, who had been waiting, in terror, in the hall.

'Clear away this soup and bring on the stew – for which all of us in this house are eternally grateful!'

He turned to Rowena. 'You're obviously not unfamiliar with the good book, Miss MacFarlane. It's a great pity that you paid less attention to its teachings than to quoting it for cheap laughs!

'At least Matthew is right in one thing. You should be told what's to become of you. I had simply wanted you to have a congenial meal first.

'This afternoon I'll take you to a refuge in Dundee, where you'll stay until your child is born. Then, no doubt, some place will be found for you, where you and the child can be together.

'Chrissie, my dear, we'll pray for Matthew, of course, but listen to me. This time I meant what I said and I *will* be obeyed.

'You'll not send him money – not a brass farthing, mind. And he can't come back into this house until he's changed his way of life. Is that clear?'

They tried, all four of them, to eat the stew which should have been tasty and nourishing, but they couldn't.

Rain filled with sleet lashed down on Dundee as the hansom cab conveying Rowena MacFarlane to the Women's Refuge negotiated its way from Camperdown to the city centre. Dundee was a fine city with some splendid buildings but the narrow streets on the outskirts were drab and dirty.

Despite the rain, barefoot children played games in the gutters which ran with muddy water and Rowena could hear the driver curse as his wheels caught in potholes.

The Reverend Walter Grey hurriedly said something to drown out the man's blasphemy, but Rowena was too anxiously watching a city that looked as sad and forlorn as she felt. Everything was dull, drab and dreary. Rowena fingered her crystal earrings for courage.

They brought Marek and his laughter closer to her. He'd told her that he had brought her the baubles from a country in the middle of Europe – a country that he claimed was the seat of their gypsy ancestors.

'Those jewels are hardly suitable for a woman in your position,' the minister's wife had remarked as Rowena had prepared to leave the Manse. 'Besides, they're sure to be stolen!'

But the glittering, multi-coloured crystals cheered Rowena and she knew they looked pretty against the blue-black gloss of her hair.

Walter Grey began to point out places of interest. 'The river – the Tay – is to our right, Rowena. It's a pity it's raining so much. Rain makes everything look, and everyone feel, dismal.'

'Don't know why. Rain brings next year's harvest, doesn't it?' Rowena replied.

Chastened, the burly minister sat back silently and let the woman look out broodingly at the mixed elegance and squalor of the city that was to be her home for the next few months.

The elegant Perth Road boasted gracious mansions with large, magnificent gardens, which, today, only looked sorry for themselves in the downpour.

But at least it was fairly quiet there. The only regular sound was the clip-clop of horses' hooves, as expensive carriages bowled along sending up sprays of cold, dirty water on rich and poor alike.

The area around Albert Square, however, even on such a day, was like bedlam. Cabs, horse buses, even the new-fangled trams all proclaimed their right to be Master of the Roads.

Newspaper-sellers dodged into doorways for some kind of protection from the elements. Despite the downpour, they still yelled their headline stories to entice possible readers.

As the hansom circled the splendidly-isolated High School, a raucous bell tolled.

It's remarkably busy for a stormy day in winter, Rowena thought, as she strained to see the forbidding building that was to house her and her unborn babe.

It was worse than she had imagined: a tall, narrow, sullen-windowed building whose stone frontage was grimed with the dirt, it seemed, of centuries, instead of less than 100 years. There were no curtains at the windows and the door ached for a coat of paint. Rowena's heart sank.

The driver reined his drooping horse to a halt and opened the door of the cab. Rowena felt her belly tighten with nervous tension.

I'll not show my fear, she vowed silently. I will not.

Mr Grey exited first and hurried up the steps to shelter under the slight overhang, while Rowena was left to the tender mercies of the driver.

'They say it's no' a bad place, lassie,' he said, his voice kindly. 'They'll no' starve you or beat you here.'

Rather wearily, poor Rowena smiled at

him and the driver stepped back, wondering what cruel fate had brought such a beautiful, almost elegant, woman to such a place.

Rowena held on to the iron railing as she climbed the steps and her stomach churned as she looked down into the basement and saw the bottles and refuse that had been thrown down there. No doubt it would be one of her duties to tidy up daily.

A scrawny maid who could have been any age between 14 and 40 opened the door to them and bobbed a nervous curtsey to the minister.

'Matron's expecting you in the parlour, yer honour,' she said and half walked, half ran ahead of them down a narrow, dark corridor.

She opened a door on the left and Rowena and her escort were almost pushed into a room.

What a difference to the general ambience of the whole building. This room was airy and well lit by a beautiful oil lamp with a multi-coloured glass shade and by the flames of a generous fire.

The Matron of the Refuge, Mrs Agnes Turnbull, was seated at a polished table on which there was a tray laden with the preparations for tea for two.

Seeing them, she rose to greet the new arrivals.

'Reverend Grey. An honour, sir. Won't you sit down?'

When she turned to Rowena, her voice hardened. 'You, MacFarlane, sit there for the moment.'

Lord, protect us all from 'good Christians' Rowena mused, as she sat listening to the Matron and the minister discussing her future as if she were no more important than a lump of coal about to be thrown on to the fire.

'I take it the man will not marry her?' the Matron was saying.

'No, he's married already, apparently. But, truth to tell, it was, by all accounts, a moment's madness on his part.'

'No doubt she led him on, Reverend.' Mrs Turnbull – a courtesy title, for she had never actually been married – leaned forward solicitously. 'We both know that men … well, some men,' she amended sycophantically, 'are weak and easily led. Will he contribute to her keep?'

Walter Grey looked over at Rowena, who sat twisting the fringe of her shawl between her strong fingers. What was she thinking?

'If he can, Mrs Turnbull.'

'Ah! His wife doesn't know then?'

Walter said nothing and Mrs Turnbull went on. 'You came at just the right time, Reverend! We haven't had an empty bed for months, but luckily Aggie Bell left last night to go into service in Broughty Ferry.

'MacFarlane may stay here until her time comes and by then we'll hope to have a job for her and a home for the child.'

Rowena tensed. 'My baby's home is with me,' she said quietly. 'We'll not be separated. Never!'

'You'll do exactly as the Board sees fit, MacFarlane!' Mrs Turnbull rang a bell furiously and a moment later the same maid as before, in her too-large apron and mob cap, entered.

'Take MacFarlane up to Dunbar's room and send Wallace in here with a tray of tea and scones.'

Walter Grey stood up and Rowena, too, stood and looked at him. She was so tall that she could look straight into his eyes and he thought, not for the first time, that the eyes were unusually direct for a woman of her type.

'Go with the maid, Rowena. You'll be well looked after here and you'll learn useful skills that'll help you when your sad trouble is behind you.' And then he disliked her again when she laughed at him showing strong white teeth.

'My *trouble?* A baby is a gift from God, Reverend. Anyway, I thank you for your hospitality and your daughter for her kindness when I was at the Manse. I'll say goodbye now.'

Rowena heard phrases like 'no shame' and 'there are some you can do nothing with, Reverend,' as the door closed behind her.

Rowena followed the little maid along the carpeted hall to a flagstoned floor. A stone staircase climbed from the flagstones to the upper floors of the house. There were no carpets here to muffle the sound of their heavy shoes.

How different from the welcoming front of the house, where it was all comfortable chairs and polished mahogany tables on which healthy foliage plants flourished.

They climbed one flight of stairs, a second, and then the maid proceeded along a wooden corridor. She stopped at the third door on the right.

'You're at the back end, so you get a look at the garden,' she said and then, as if ashamed that she had shown so much humanity, she threw open the door and almost pushed Rowena inside.

The room was not much bigger than the outside wash-house at Springhill Farm and was almost as uncomfortable. There were two iron bedsteads, one pushed against the wall and the other almost under the window.

There was one wooden chair and one two-drawer chest. There was nothing at all on the whitewashed walls. Of her room-mate,

Dunbar, there was no sign.

Rowena put her bag on the floor and sat down on the chair. She closed her eyes for a second and then opened them quickly as the smell of unwashed body fought with the smell of overcooked cabbage, which had filled the staircase and corridors.

She went over to the window. Good grief, was this supposed to be more pleasant than the front of the house? The 'garden' consisted of a drying green, a wash-house and an outhouse.

There was a tree beside the wall at the bottom of the garden and perhaps there would be blossom of some kind in the spring. Now, though, it looked as sad as Rowena felt.

She was suddenly deathly tired and would have liked to lie down, but which bed was hers and which belonged to the missing Dunbar?

She was not left in doubt for long. The door opened suddenly and a woman who had obviously seen better days entered.

'So you're MacFarlane,' she said. 'Well, I'm Ruby Dunbar and I'm to take you down for your tea.

'No' that it's much. Just two slices of bread and dripping, but at least you'll get two cups of tea since wee Hazel's serving – that's if the Queen of Sheba doesnae come along tae hae another look at you!

'That's my bed under the window by the way, and the top drawer's mine. No' that I have much to put in it.' She looked at Rowena's bag. 'Looks as if you've as many clothes as the gentry.'

'Hardly! I have another skirt, some underclothes, a nightgown, and a Sunday shawl – that's it!' Rowena protested.

At the sound of her voice, Dunbar started. 'You're no' Irish, are you? I hope no'! We're no' over fond of the Irish here.'

'I'm Romany,' Rowena explained proudly and laughed to herself when she saw that Dunbar didn't have a clue what she meant, but hesitated to show it.

'Ay, weel, as long as you're no' Irish! Come on, leave your bag on your bed and let's get down for our tea. There's some here as would scoff it as soon as look at you!'

The smell of the cabbage accompanied them downstairs and, as they neared the kitchen, a smell that Rowena finally identified as burnt potato joined it.

The dining-hall was a cold, white-washed room, which contained an oak sideboard and a large, scrubbed table around which were clustered several chairs, most of which had seen better days. There were women in the chairs, women who, like the chairs, badly needed some care and attention.

The wee maid who had taken Rowena upstairs was waving a heavy teapot around dangerously, simply because it was too heavy for her scrawny wrist.

A dinner plate covered with an upended tin plate had been placed in front of one of the empty chairs.

'Hazel's saved our tea for us,' Ruby said triumphantly, sitting down in the less rickety of the two empty chairs.

A wave of nausea hit Rowena and she grabbed for the back of the chair. She could not sit here with these women, one or two of whom looked as if they should be in the madhouse instead of the Refuge.

What had happened to these women to bring them here? Neglect, cruelty, mental and physical abuse and, no doubt, in one or two cases, their own wrong doing. Rowena knew that somehow, no matter what, she had to get out of here.

'Sit down, lass,' Ruby instructed, grasping her hand in a claw-like grip. 'There's no favours down here. If you leave the table, they'll eat your tea.

'This is Rowena,' she announced casually, as she took the tin plate off their bread, 'and, as you can see, she's eating for two – so lay off her, right?'

Rowena sat down. Hazel managed to get the cups almost full of tea and she pushed the sugar bowl towards Rowena with a bizarre grimace that Rowena eventually recognised as a smile.

No-one spoke, but their eyes never left their examination of Rowena's face while she tried to eat her supper.

Back at Springhill Farm, Tam Laird had noted that Rowena no longer worked in the farmhouse. It was the Campbell boys who told him.

'Nobody tells us stories any more,' wee Jamie said sadly. 'Weena was brilliant at that.'

'Well, your mammy's too busy, laddie. She'll get a new lass at the next Feein' Market and maybe then she'll have time for stories.'

'They'll no' be as good as Rowena's,' Colin commented. 'Hers were all about wizards and dragons...'

'And kings and beautiful princesses,' wee James interrupted. 'I love Rowena; I think she's a princess. She said she was.'

Colin looked at Tam man to man. 'He's still only a baby,' he remarked with all the authority his extra months gave him.

Tam was not so sure. Children, he felt, were astute guides of human nature.

'Well, you should both away in for your tea,' he said. 'I have Fern here to take inside.' He did not want to tell the boys that his beloved Clydesdale mare was due to drop her foal in a few days and he was eager to get her back into her warm, comfortable stall.

'I made a slide today, Tam. Everybody tried it, even auld Harry. Do you want a shot?'

'Ach, I think I'm a wee bit too old for sliding on the ice, Colin. Where did you make your slide? No' in the steading I hope?'

'Em, well, it *was* there but Duddy made us move it. He said folk might fall. So we made a new one out on the road. It's a belter!'

'Ay, it's the longest slide anybody's ever seen, Tam,' James enthused. 'You'll have to have a turn. Daddy did and he lifted me and we fell. It didn't hurt, though, 'cause he was underneath.'

Tam laughed. 'Isn't that what daddies are for? To make sure you have soft landings! Right, boys, I'll give it a try but after I've got Fern in, all right? It's getting too dark for sliding the day.'

In November and December it had seemed as if there would never be enough light for the work that had to be done. But the days of January and now February were stretching longer and longer into the evening.

By the end of February, you should be able to read *The Courier* on Reform Street at six in the evening. So said the old wives' tale and it seemed to be true.

'Give us a ride in on Fern, Tam. We'll be late if you don't.'

'I cannae, lambies. I still have work to do

here – you'd better run on so your mam disnae fret.'

The little boys stroked the horse's soft nose one last time and then turned and ran home as fast as all their winter woollies would allow.

Meanwhile, Tam went on with his work methodically until it was done.

It never occurred to him to stop at five-thirty, which was when his word of mouth contract said he should finish in February. He lived by his own code and finished working, summer and winter, when his daily tasks were done and not a moment before.

It was growing pretty dark when he and the stately Fern made their proud but slow way home. The moon and stars had not yet found their way through the clouds that lined the winter sky. Tam could feel Fern's breath warm on his neck as he walked just under her shoulder and he smiled.

'Better nor a muffler any day, lass!' he said – and Fern's soft blowing was the last thing he remembered...

Lizzie Campbell had melted her sons' slide and scattered ashes from the great kitchen range on the ground to make sure that there was no danger to man or beast. But not even Lizzie could melt all the ice on the Angus roads.

The boys had been furious to see their

'brilliant' slide destroyed, but the thaw had not come during the day and, though they said nothing, the children looked eagerly forward to the morning when they might start again.

They were sitting at the kitchen table spooning up Lizzie's delicious smoked haddock soup when the whole house shook with a force that terrified even Angus.

'What in the name of the Almighty was that?'

The four of them, Angus, Lizzie and the children stared at one another for a long, frightened moment. Then Angus reached for Jamie, whose big eyes looked set to pop from his head with the fright of the terrifying noise.

But it was Colin who screamed, a scream that Lizzie felt she would remember till the last breath left her body.

'It's Fern! It's Fern – I know it!'

Angus shook his oldest son hard. 'Be quiet, lad, you're frightening your wee brother!' Angus was at the door reaching for his coat, his hat, his scarf.

'It's more like a cart's crashed into the barn, or those daft loons in the Bothy have been up to no good. I'll no' be long...'

He rushed outside, firmly closing the door behind him, praying, hoping against all hope that he would not see what he knew he was going to see.

It was worse than Angus Campbell had expected. It seemed that Tam had tried to shore up the slipping mare and had fallen under the full, crushing weight of the frightened horse.

The agonised squealing from the animal was a sound that Angus, too, would carry with him for the rest of his life.

But worse than the noise from the horse was the terrifying silence from his first horseman...

Angus fell to his knees beside them, one hand on the horse's neck in a vain attempt to quieten her, the other desperately examining, as far as he dared, the body of the man.

'Help me, John,' he begged his second horseman, who had just arrived with others from the Bothy and was standing, mouth open in horror, unable to deal with what he was seeing. 'Come on, John lad, help me slide Tam out from under the mare.

'Harry, you go in and get my gun off the wall in the parlour. Quick now! And send the loon off for the doctor.'

Auld Harry, the third horseman, who'd worked on the farm even longer than Angus himself, hurried away.

John, happier that he now had an order to obey, closed his mouth and knelt down on the icy road beside his employer. 'The lad's away, Maister – but you'll no' shoot Fern, will you?'

'I'll shoot you if you don't stop moaning! Get ready now, John – I'll lift and you slide Tam out.'

'You'll no' be able to lift that weight,' John began, but Angus Campbell had summoned superhuman strength from somewhere and had eased the huge shoulders of the struggling horse from the slight figure who lay crushed and still beneath it.

John tried to move Tam Laird as gently as he could while the veins stood out on Angus's forehead from the effort of holding the struggling horse. Slowly, slowly Tam was eased free.

Together they looked at Tam, then Angus put his ear against his face to check if there was breath.

'He's alive, John – but I daren't move him. There's no' a mark on him. That's when it's dangerous. We'll get blankets and wrap him up warm here and maybe get him a hot-water bottle. Tell the mistress to take it from our bed.

'Damn it, where's that auld fool with the gun? I can't bear to hear this horse screamin'!'

'Don't, Maister. You'll kill the foal and all, and it's Gavin's Boy's! A champion for sure. Tam would be...'

But the words tailed off, as John couldn't

think how to finish his sentence about his well-respected boss.

Just then the farmhouse door opened and light and old Harry spilled out together.

Angus looked and saw that there was no gun and, cursing under his breath, he ran to the door himself.

'We couldnae find the cartridges, Maister,' Harry explained apologetically. 'The mistress said you put them away where the boys wouldnae find them...'

There was no point in yelling at the old man or at Lizzie. Instead, Angus stayed quite calm as he fetched his gun and loaded it. Turning to go out again, he was stopped by his children, who threw their arms about his knees.

Angrily, he pushed them off, his heart beating wildly. His finger had been on the trigger of the loaded shotgun. Had he fallen...

Oh, where was the damn doctor? Tam was in desperate need of help ... before it was too late.

'Go to your mother, boys,' he tried to speak gently. 'Daddy's busy now.'

'Don't shoot Tam, Daddy, even though he's broken!' Colin sobbed, his small arms once more tight around his father's knees.

Colin was a farmer born and bred. This would not be the first time he had seen his father shoot an injured animal, but his terror was for Tam, his wonderful friend, who was also badly hurt.

Did Daddies shoot men who were broken, too?

'Lizzie!' Angus, at the end of his tether, yelled for her assistance. And for once, Lizzie, without a word, hurried from the scullery and pried her son from his father.

Sadly, Colin's delay did not save Fern, who died as she expelled her foal into the freezing air. The orramen had worked as fast as they could to pile straw around the struggling Clydesdale as soon as John Smith had realised that Nature had taken over and that the dying mare was in labour.

Only auld Harry sat on the cold ground, holding Tam's hand and sobbing out a mixture of prayer to the Almighty and oaths levelled against whoever or whatever was responsible for the long, cold spell.

At last, the doctor arrived in his trap and soon Tam was on the way to the Royal Infirmary in faraway Dundee, a 16-mile journey made worse by poor roads and no lights.

'It's futile,' the doctor said mournfully, shaking his head. 'You'd have done Tam a favour if you'd put a bullet in him, too, Angus.'

'Just you keep telling him that Fern's had her foal. A grand wee filly,' Angus replied. 'I'll see to my wife and children first, then

I'll come to Dundee. Put me down as his next of kin – and whatever Tam needs, get it for him.'

The doctor shook his head again. They expected him to be a miracle worker and then complained because he was a mere human with no supernatural gifts. 'The surgeons will do everything they can, Angus, but...'

There was no point in adding that he was sure that their best would not be good enough. Tam Laird was strong and wiry but a pregnant Clydesdale had fallen on top of him.

Maybe a bullet *would* have been the kindest way out for him...

Walter Grey sat at the meagre fire in the Manse study and rubbed his cold hands together. He remembered the generous fire in the Matron's room at the Woman's Refuge and he hoped, without too much faith, that the fires in the residents' quarters blazed as merrily.

The gypsy woman would be near her time now and he was glad that she was in respectable and safe surroundings.

It wasn't exactly a comfortable home, but better than a gypsy campfire, or worse, a hedgerow somewhere...

The door opened and his wife, Chrissie, came in with the cocoa. He was pleased to see that there were two cups and saucers and two biscuits on the plate.

She had avoided him for weeks. That was a strange thing to say about the woman who shared his table and his bed, but it was amazing how far you could be from someone whose body was in the same room

'Walter, I have to ask you something,' Chrissie began and he saw that her hands were trembling as she poured the cocoa. 'It's about Matthew. Listen, I can't take any more of this. Where is he, Walter? Where is my son?'

The guilty feelings he had struggled to stifle surfaced again, as Walter took the cup from his wife's hands. He, a minister, a man of God, had thrown his own son out into a cold, inhospitable world.

If only the boy had pleaded instead of standing there on the doorstep in his thin evening clothes with that disparaging look on his handsome face...

'I won't come back like the Prodigal son begging for a crust, sir. You know that, don't you?'

And, goaded, Walter had shouted. 'You wouldn't get a crumb here even if you did, you wastrel. If you want to eat, then get a job!'

By finding her a place in the Women's Refuge, he had done more for Rowena MacFarlane than he had for his own son.

129

That was the irony of it.

Enough of that, though. His duty was done there.

'I don't know where Matthew is, my dear. No doubt he's with friends. We'd have heard if anything untoward had happened to him.'

'I keep trying to believe that.' Chrissie put down her cup and knelt like a penitent at his feet. 'The weather has been so bad, Walter. He could be dead in a ditch somewhere for all we know.'

Embarrassed by the unwarranted and unexpected show of sentiment, Walter lifted his wife to her feet.

'Chrissie, men like our son always find a place. I'm sorry I lost my temper with him. I forgot my cloth, but I was sorely tried.

'The truth is, we have given Matthew everything – and more – than we could afford and we're paying for it now. He will come back to us, though, like the Prodigal son. I know he will. This silence is just because he wants me to squirm, to suffer...'

'And if he doesn't come back, Walter? If something really has happened?'

'Listen, he'll be fine. He's looking for employment and he'll come back, as I told him to, when he's found it.'

'He took his books.'

'See! Didn't I tell you there was no need to worry? Perhaps he's decided to sell them to help support him for a day or two.'

'He's gone for a soldier, hasn't he?'

That, too, had been worrying Walter. As a child, Matthew had always said that he wanted the type of adventure that an army career was supposed to offer.

Now, not for the first time, the Reverend Walter Grey found himself in the position of not being quite truthful.

'Matthew hasn't the money to be an officer and he'd never sign on as an enlisted man. He likes comfort too much.

'Chrissie, he'll be back when he's convinced himself that you'll be so worried that I'll forgive him everything.

'Our son is weak. You must be strong.'

The Greys would have been surprised to see their son and the farmer Campbell on the same errand.

Matt, who had found cheap lodgings in a rooming-house, could not get pictures of Rowena MacFarlane out of his mind: weak and exhausted in her rags as his arms had supported her; then bathed and dressed in clean clothes with her magnificent hair tied back from the white column of her throat and her eyes, flashing at him as she teased, equal to equal.

Who *was* the father of her child? He could not believe her uniqueness. She must have had real affection, perhaps misplaced, for the man. And how long would her vibrant beauty last if she were not rescued?

He had been stunned by Rowena's physical appearance. Probably, never in her life, had she looked so wonderful and it was doubtful if she would ever reach that dizzy height of perfection again.

Her natural beauty had been definitely enhanced by her pregnancy.

She'd looked soft and gentle and there was an exquisite bloom about her cheeks.

She was not a small woman yet she'd looked vulnerable, and somehow strong and delicate at the same time.

Matt had wanted to gather her up in his arms to protect her.

Now he shied away from what he was beginning to feel and decided to take her some books to read. It was a genuinely charitable gesture – the stamp of the Manse must be on him still...

He certainly did not expect to see Angus Campbell, a sack of potatoes on his strong shoulders, at the door before him, and Matt stood well back until the farmer had gone in.

Hazel, the same wee maid who'd greeted Rowena, admitted him.

'Matron's busy at the moment. You'll have to wait,' she said, showing Matt to a seat in the polished hall.

He waited until she had disappeared behind the door that separated the front of the house from the residents' quarters and then, quite calmly, put his ear to the door. But it was thick and he could hear only murmuring.

He did not want Campbell to see him, so when the maid, no doubt summoned, came back into the hall, he slipped past her frightened form and stood just behind the door.

'But Mistress Turnbull, wouldn't...' Hazel began.

'Just do as you're bid,' Matt whispered urgently, charming the girl with a smile. 'Take Mr Campbell to see MacFarlane. He was her employer, you see, and feels some responsibility.'

Matt followed them at a discreet distance. The maid led Angus upstairs, and then along an uncarpeted corridor to Rowena's room, where she left him and went on to the servants' stairs at the back.

Matt waited until she was gone and then tiptoed to the door. He could hear Rowena speaking urgently.

'The baby's coming soon and then they're planning to send me away. But I'll tell you now – I will *not* be separated from my child!'

'No, no, Rowena, you won't be. I promised you. One third of everything I own belongs to the bairn.'

'Ay, well, it'll be no use if the child's stuck in an orphanage.'

'No son of mine will grow up in a charity home. That's a promise...'

Stunned by what Angus had just said, Matt waited to hear no more.

'No son of mine...'

Keeping as quiet as he could, he slipped back down the stairs. At last, he reached the thick carpet that muffled his footsteps.

Rowena could do without the books for a day or two. He needed to think hard about what he had just heard. There had to be a way to make the information work for both Rowena and himself.

Angus Campbell would hardly want that prune-faced wife of his to know that he had fathered a gypsy child...

When the fates deal a good hand, the wise man plays it!

Tam Laird lay silent and still in the long ward at Dundee Infirmary. He heard nothing, felt nothing. The consultants walked past him and automatically lowered their voices and the nurses sped past on rubber-soled shoes and, when they had time, wondered if he would give up his fight today.

For eventually he would lose – he could not win – and they needed the bed.

One by one, when they could, the horsemen from Springhill Farm came and sat nervously by the bed.

John Smith, second horseman visited more than any, for he felt guilty. Of course, he wanted Tam to recover; of course he did... But if Tam did not...

John saw a glorious future for himself. Imagine – John Smith, first horseman, number one. If he were head horseman, he could ask the boss to redd up that wee cottage near the wood and he could maybe ask a lassie to marry him.

A good job and a house was what a man needed before he could marry, and lying here on the hospital bed was the only person between him and his dream.

He saw Tam's eyelids fluttering. 'Did you hear me, Tam?' he said forgetting ambition for the moment. 'We managed to save Fern's foal. She's a topper. You've got yourself another wee champion.'

But Tam was still again and the consultant came and said, 'Yes, it's possible that something's going on in there – but only time will tell.'

They really say things like that, John thought to himself. Only time will tell if Tam dies and I get his job. Who's to say I'd get it anyway...

Rowena was looking everywhere for her earrings. She had worn them defiantly every day and every night she had carefully put them in the pocket of her dress that lay across the bottom of her bed.

This morning, however, they were not there.

'You're no' accusing me of taking them!' Ruby shouted before Rowena had time to say anything other than that they'd gone.

'Let's just say they were in my pocket last night and they're not there this morning. If I get them back, we'll forget it ever happened.'

'Will we indeed, Madame Hoity Toity? No Irish tinker who's no better than she should be is going to come in here and accuse me of being a thief.'

'But you are,' said wee Hazel the maid, who had come in to tell them there would be no porridge left if they didn't get a move on. 'Everybody knows that, Ruby.'

She turned to the pregnant inmate. 'She's been inside for pinchin' three times, Rowena. Then she gets out and her man beats her senseless for getting caught!'

With an animal screech of rage, Ruby hurled herself at Hazel.

'I'll get you for that, you wee–! I'll sort you!' she screamed and punched Hazel to the floor.

Then they were rolling around on the floor, biting and scratching like wild animals.

Rowena stood for a second, shocked by the unexpected violence, then she bent down and tried to separate them.

'Stop it!' she yelled, but her protest was useless.

They were beyond hearing, beyond caring, only the desire to inflict pain on the opponent was important to them.

Exasperated, Rowena bent down to try to force them apart, just as Ruby freed her legs and kicked wildly at Hazel...

Rowena took the full force of the angry blow in her midriff. She sat down abruptly but she had effectively stopped the fight.

Two tear-stained faces gazed at her.

'You're no' hurt, are you, lassie?' Ruby asked, appalled.

'No, she's fine. Just a bit winded,' Hazel added, her expression a study in anxiety.

'You're right, I'm fine,' Rowena began and then her belly was suddenly gripped by a pain that took her completely by surprise. It was as if a pair of red-hot pincers had gripped her stomach and been squeezed by a giant hand...

She moaned once and slumped, unconscious to the floor.

Hours later, Ruby knelt by the window in their room and pried up the floorboard nearest to the wall. This was her secret place. She hid bread in there or an apple, sometimes even a bone from a chop. You never knew in this life where your next meal was coming from, especially if you had been stupid enough to marry a man like her Harry.

'You know you're just exchanging your brute of a faither for another one like him,' her mam had said, but when did girls ever listen to their mothers?

Harry had kicked her once during her one and only pregnancy, just as she had kicked Rowena, but, please God, she hadn't meant it and Harry had.

He had known he would destroy the baby and if he had been told there could never be another, which was true, he would not have cared.

But she had nothing against Rowena, even though she was a black-eyed Irish tinker with her grand tales of Romany royalty and such nonsense.

Ah, there they were! They were so pretty. The sun made the crystal stones sparkle like diamonds.

Ruby held the earrings against her breast just once, then shoved them into the pocket of her apron.

She would give them back to the tinker – for her baby. For word had it that the bairn and the mother would both be all right.

She would even say she was sorry and maybe, just maybe, Rowena would let her hold the baby when the time came. She would hold it as if it were the most precious thing in the whole world, which it was.

Would it smile at her and not notice the broken nose and the scars, or would it be frightened like everyone else? Most folk dismissed her with words like, 'Nasty piece of jail meat, that Ruby.'

No, Ruby decided, Rowena was not like that and her baby would not be like that either. She really had meant them no harm.

If Rowena would let her – and she would pray as she had not prayed since she was a child for that – Ruby Dunbar vowed that she would serve them both all the days of her life.

Would this child never be born? Rowena lay on the narrow bed and moaned in agony. Never, ever, had she imagined that childbirth would be like this...

After the spat between Hazel and Ruby, there had been concern for the infant, but eventually any danger had passed.

Now the bairn's time had come...

The intense spasm passed and she lay back in relief.

The midwife wiped the sweat from Rowena's face. 'Relax, lassie! You're far too tense and that's what makes it hurt.'

Rowena stared blankly at the midwife. She

had heard sounds, but had not understood the words. And then another fierce contraction, worse than the one before, gripped her and her pain-racked body tried to curl itself up, as if against a blow.

Someone grabbed her bare feet. 'Oh, don't do that, Rowena! Just lie still. There, there, it'll be all right.'

That voice. She recognised it, but could not remember whose it was; a gentle, diffident voice.

'Relax, just relax,' the first voice soothed again.

Hearing it, Rowena rebelled against its note of authority.

Relax? How could she relax when Nature – or whatever it was – was tearing her apart?

'I can't, you idiot!' she moaned. 'I'm having a baby!' A baby, a real living baby, who seemed intent on destruction as he struggled to be born.

Before the midwife could reply, Rowena screamed again, a scream that made the hair stand up on the back of wee Hazel's neck – for it was the little maid who had been ordered to help with the delivery.

Rowena threshed her head from side to side in a desperate attempt to get away from the pain. She had to break free; she had to. But how?

She yelled again, the howl rising like a distressed animal's from the back of her throat, forcing her clamped teeth open.

'There's definitely something no' right here, Mrs Thomson!' Hazel stressed, shivering with fright. 'You'll need to get the doctor.'

'And you're going to pay his fee, are you?' the midwife asked gruffly. She knew that a doctor would only be called out if it were absolutely necessary.

'I think the bairn's in breech. I'll have to try to turn it. Right, you hold her hands, Hazel, to keep her from falling off the bed.'

Hazel leaned across Rowena's writhing form and clasped her hands. 'Rowena, hang on to me,' she said softly. 'Your baby's coming.'

But Rowena was past hearing or understanding. As the worried midwife began to try to turn the baby, the gypsy girl was hit by more agony than even she could bear.

To Hazel's relief, this time, Rowena fainted.

The mother-to-be surfaced again as the baby, at last correctly positioned, decided to make its entrance into the world.

Rowena felt an overwhelming desire to push. She did so – and her child was born.

The midwife did what was necessary and then put the infant, screaming lustily, into the exhausted mother's waiting arms.

Hazel looked on in awe as, all pain

forgotten, Rowena's fingers gently traced the child's face.

'My wee "lad" is a lass, Hazel! I'm so happy. To be honest, that's what I wanted all the time.'

Hazel was so moved by the miracle she had just witnessed that she could barely speak. 'Have you a name for her?' she managed at last.

Rowena lay back against the pillow, holding her daughter in the crook of her arm. She was tired, so tired, and she wanted to drift away from the exhaustion and pain into healing sleep. She managed to smile.

'Ishbel,' she said and the voice was a blessing. 'My precious wee Ishbel.'

The birch trees stood like trusty sentinels as the caravans slept. The birches witnessed the stealthy approach of the villagers but they could do nothing to warn the gypsies.

Marek's huge dog, Thane, lay sleeping under the steps of a yellow caravan, his legs twitching as he relived a successful rabbit hunt. But then some instinct alerted him and he was suddenly wide awake, his hair bristling up all along his backbone.

Thane could smell them. He barked furiously, both to wake Marek and to frighten off the intruders, then he launched himself into the open.

At the same time, Marek himself appeared, half dressed in the doorway. Behind him was Pheemie Stewart, proud, independent – and obviously in love with the swarthy, well-muscled man before her.

Men were rushing from other caravans. Anxious dogs were barking and snapping ferociously...

The women stood in the doorways calling encouragement to their menfolk and trying to prevent small children from getting caught up in the mêlée.

It wasn't often that the bad blood between the villagers and the gypsies erupted into violence, but when it did the action was fast, furious and bloody.

Marek's mother, the matriarch of the gypsy band, stood with her shotgun at the ready, more as a deterrent than anything else.

She was sure that Marek would resolve this situation quickly and decisively. He was, after all, his late father's son and had inherited all the qualities required of a powerful, respected leader.

Antagonism had been simmering for weeks. The gypsies' arrival in the woods had coincided with the disappearance of a load of firewood which had been stacked outside a house in the village. Soon afterwards, a delegation of villagers had come to see Marek.

'We've come for our logs.'

'You'll find no stolen logs here,' Marek assured the man calmly.

'No, but only because you've burned them already, you thieving tinkers!' one of the irate villagers snapped.

Marek did not allow his anger to show. Instead, he shrugged nonchalantly.

'Well then, you can prove nothing,' he pointed out, adding, 'but why on earth should we steal firewood when it's lying all over the forest floor? It's free for lifting, so why should we cause trouble?'

The men had left then, muttering angrily.

A few days later, however, a fine fat hen had disappeared from a back garden coop.

'One hen, even a fine fat one, wouldn't go far among so many of us,' Marek had argued when his accusers had returned. 'I can only suggest that you look to your own folk first.'

A week later, it was a goose which made so much noise as it was carried off that its owner had heard the commotion and looked from his window to see. 'A thieving tinker,' he'd muttered.

And, unfortunately, according to the aggrieved owner, the thief had got away with the goose.

Now, as dawn broke, the pent-up frustrations on both sides were being released as violent kicks and blows were exchanged. The clearing rang with cries of pain, anger and fear. As the enemies wrestled and struggled, it was difficult to tell who was friend, who was foe.

Marek who had been rallying all his men with great courage and vigour was suddenly floored by a cowardly blow from someone who had sneaked up on him with a pick axe handle.

Stunned, he lay on the ground for a moment, waiting for his head to stop ringing. When he groggily opened his eyes, he saw, to his horror, flames dancing before him.

Dizziness ignored, he sprang to his feet like a greyhound from the slips.

'Fire! Fire!' he shrieked, as he ran through the mêlée to his mother's caravan.

The matriarch stood, her shotgun at the ready, unaware of the flames that licked at the curtains of her gaily-painted, yellow caravan.

'Mother, get away from there!' Marek yelled, as the hungry fire raced across the wooden shutters and up on to the roof.

Perhaps she felt the heat and heard her son's cry at the same time, for she turned, stumbled, and pitched forward off the steps.

The 12-bore went off as it hit the ground, and the noise reverberated around the camp.

When the eerie echoes of the explosion died, the words were silent again – even the birds made not a sound.

Marek knelt by his mother's crumpled body and the other gypsies and the villagers – their differences forgotten – gathered around in horrified, concerned silence.

All who saw, knew that the worse had happened. To the Romanies, something vital, wise and revered had been snatched away from them... 'And all for a goose we did not steal.'

Clutching his mother to him, Marek whispered, unnecessarily, 'She's gone. My mother is dead.'

Then he let out a yell that expressed all the grief and anger and frustration that boiled within himself.

After a moment or two, Pheemie dared to put her hand on his bowed head. 'Marek,' she implored, 'remember the living, my love – the fire! It's spreading!'

The gypsies and villagers now worked together to douse the flames and to pull the wagons to safety. No-one spoke. No instructions were needed.

Side by side, they worked like brothers and, at last, the fires were extinguished with only the yellow wagon destroyed.

'Maybe the old woman was boiling water...' the leader of the villagers suggested tentatively, anxious that the village would not be blamed for a suspicious death.

'No, all our cooking is done outside,' Marek replied, reliving in his mind that moment when his mother had stumbled and fallen. 'Her death was an accident and the blame for it lies as much at my door as yours. But she did not set fire to her own wagon, that's for certain.'

'A candle maybe?' a villager suggested desperately.

'It started at the curtains, Marek,' Pheemie said softly.

Marek shook his head as if to shake away the grief, the pain, the futility. 'What does it matter? We'll have to get out of here now ... too much sorrow.'

'Where will we go?'

'To the north,' he said quietly. 'To Forfar. To anywhere.'

To where Rowena MacFarlane is, Pheemie thought, her heart beating quicker. His feelings for Rowena obviously blazed inside him yet – a fire that nothing could put out...

Matthew Grey had been staying at a rooming-house in Dundee and had eventually found a job as a night porter in a seedy hotel. He hated the work and loathed his room, especially the horsehair mattress, in which countless families of fleas lived happily together raising countless armies of offspring.

He was determined to leave both as soon as something better turned up.

He thought about his parents and his home in the Manse, where there had always been enough food and where cleanliness was taken for granted and for the first time in his life he was ashamed.

His father was right. He had thrown away everything and he vowed to try to claw himself back into his father's esteem if not his affection.

Affectionate thoughts turned his mind to Rowena MacFarlane yet again. In fact, he was amazed at how often an image of her face, her beautiful face, would flash into his thoughts.

'Heads you'll go, tails you won't,' he muttered to himself, as he sat at the desk in the hotel tossing a coin, his last coin.

Heads.

'Damn! For once, I think I actually wanted to lose,' Matt said out loud. He shrugged and began to plan his campaign.

Wednesday was his day off and before he took the horse bus out to Springhill Farm, he went to visit Rowena at the Women's Refuge.

But Hazel, the maid, turned him away. 'She's just had a wee lassie,' she explained, her eyes shining at the wonder of it. 'She won't be allowed up for another week.'

She flushed a bright purply red. She was

so excited by the baby lying upstairs in a drawer taken out of a dresser that she had been about to confide secrets of Rowena's medical condition.

'She's fine, though,' she said instead. 'Just a wee bit tired.'

'Well, could you tell her I called and that I'll come back next week? Maybe she'll be able to see me then.'

Hazel nodded as she closed the door. Fancy having a handsome, well-set young man like that coming to call.

'Mind you, you'll be lucky if her and wee Ishbel's still here,' she told the wooden panels of the door, but Matt, of course, could not hear her.

He had walked off towards the High Street to catch a horse bus. He would not go home, not yet. First he had to find himself a better-paid job and he thought he knew exactly how to get it...

At Springhill Farm, Mrs Campbell told Matt that her husband was in the burn feeding the new filly. She said she would send down for him, though.

Matt smiled at her, the smile he knew that few, if any, women had ever been able to resist.

'No, no, don't disturb him if he's busy, Mistress. I can wait – as long as he's home before the last Dundee bus passes the end

149

of the road.'

Lizzie smiled back at him. 'Oh, of course he will be! It's just the one wee horse, Mr Grey. Meantime, come in and I'll make you a cup of tea while you're waiting.'

Lizzie Campbell was not quite sure how much truth there was in the rumour flying around about the goings-on at the old manse and she was delighted to have an opportunity to find out for herself – but Matt was too clever and too sophisticated for her.

She had no idea how to bring the conversation round to his estrangement from his family and Matt had no intention of helping her. Neither did he tell her why he wanted to speak to her husband.

Even when Angus got back from the barn, she had to cool her heels in the kitchen while the two men talked.

Angus knew a visit from Matthew Grey would not be a pleasurable thing for him and his feelings and worries were so close to the surface that he refused to waste time in idle chatter.

'Why are you here, lad? You're not living at the Manse now so you're obviously not here on your father's business.'

Matt was glad to get down to brass tacks right away.

'Well, the thing is, I have a job of sorts, Angus, at a dreadful hotel in Dundee. But I honestly think I'd prefer dumb animals to dumb human beings.

'Perhaps there's something here that would suit me? I hear your first horseman's pretty bad...'

Angus had been looking at his minister's son in growing consternation. At this latest, outrageous comment, he exploded.

'And you plan to take Tam Laird's place? Tam Laird, the finest horseman in the county, if not the whole of Scotland! Do you actually think you could do his job?'

'Not at all. I admit I know nothing, absolutely nothing, about horses, but I'm willing to learn. Anyway, surely there must be something that I can do around here? Anything would be better than lifting drunks out of the gutter and carrying them up to flea-ridden rooms.

'I'm sure you'd agree, Angus, that that isn't a proper job for the son of the Manse, especially a son of this particular manse.'

'I'm sorry, but there's nothing for you here, Matt,' Angus said firmly. 'A horseman's a skilled worker and I can't afford to carry any dead weight.'

'Not much skill needed to shift bales of hay.'

'The halflins, the boys, do that. I'm not paying a man's wages for a job a growing lad can do while he's training.'

Matt got up and walked to the fireplace.

151

He laughed, but his laughter was directed against himself. He found he could not look directly at the man he was about to blackmail.

'Em, I hear that Rowena MacFarlane has given birth to a bonny wee girl.'

Angus started up out of his chair.

'A girl, did you say? A wee girl?' he repeated in awe. Then he collected himself. 'Well, what's that to me or mine, Matt?'

Matt smiled, but it was not the pleasant, open smile with which he had rewarded Lizzie Campbell for her fresh-baked scones.

'Why nothing, Angus. Why should it mean anything to you?'

The farmer went to the door. He was trying to feel relief. But he did not trust Matthew Grey.

'Well, I'll bid you good day. We've nothing more to say to one another,' he said.

Matt Grey walked across the big room towards him. 'As you wish, Angus, I'll just stop in the kitchen to thank Mistress Campbell for the lovely cup of tea she made me. Oh, and while I'm there, I'll tell her all about a conversation I overheard the other day in the Women's Refuge.

'Very enlightening, it was – a bit distressing, though. She'll be fascinated. Concerns the new baby's father...'

Angus felt the blood drain from his veins and he closed the door and leaned against it for a moment, his eyes closed.

Sadly, when he opened them again, Matt Grey was still there and that blasted smile was still on his handsome face. The boy knew the truth.

How, Angus had no idea, but he had no alternative but to agree to his demands.

'Well, now that I've had time to think, Matt, there might just be some work you could turn your hand to. That would free up a trained man to help Tam Laird when he's better.'

'Fine, but there's a bit more to my proposition, Angus...'

Tam Laird was recovering. It was going to take a long time. Broken bones had to knit, but a broken bone was nothing. It was the internal damage that was causing the main worries.

It never occurred to Tam that his employer was as afraid of losing him as he was of losing his job. As soon as he was conscious, Tam waited for the dreaded visitor who would tell him that Horseman Number Two had become Horseman Number One.

For the first time in his life, he regretted that he had not made time to find a wife. If he had a wife and a home, he would not be lying here sweating with the fear of destitution.

Would he ever walk again? Could he ever

train up a horse to where his Fern had been – or Gavin's Boy? He worried that Gavin's Boy was not being handled properly.

Och, he'd be fed and groomed right enough but that was not nearly enough when you were working a good horse. Rapport had to build up, slowly, steadily. No hasty hand should be dealing with Gavin's Boy.

And then there was the filly he hadn't even seen – Fern's daughter, as sweet and gentle as her mother, by all accounts, and as intelligent and sensitive as her father.

Tam fretted to get well.

'You're your own worst enemy, Tam,' his ward nurse told him time and again. 'Relax, man! There are some things you can't rush.'

But Tam had to rush to get well. Otherwise he'd end up a broken man in a workhouse. He *had* to get well.

'Hello, Tam. How you doin' the day?'

Tam opened his eyes and tried to look pleased when he saw his employer looking down at him.

At least he had come in person to tell him he had been replaced.

Angus Campbell pulled up the chair by the bed and sat down. 'Right, Tam, the doctors tell me you're well enough to talk about the future. It seems it'll be a wee while yet afore you're winning blue ribbons all over the county.'

'Ay, Maister, but I'll be there some time. I'm gettin' a wee bit better every day.'

'Well, Mrs Campbell and I don't want you to worry about a thing, Tam.'

Angus remembered Lizzie's anger when he had told her that Tam Laird would need months of careful nursing, nursing that could not possibly be done in the bothy, no matter how willing the men were.

'As soon as you're well enough, you're coming back to the farm.'

Looking at the younger man, Tam wanted to lie to him, but he had never lied in his life.

'Best no' be too hasty, Maister. They tell me it'll be at least a year afore I can handle a horse again a *year* that is.'

'Tam Laird, do you think for one moment that I'd let the best horseman in Scotland go? My God, man, are they not queuing up outside the infirmary to hire you! No, seriously, we want you to come back to Springhill, Tam.

'There's a wee cottage in the Low Pasture that I'll get made weatherproof. If you'd been a married man, it would've been done when I hired you.

'The first horseman's entitled to his own fireside.'

Though his heart was racing, Tam did not give in to relief. Maybe Angus Campbell did not understand just how much nursing he would need. No-one would hire him in his present state. He would be useless for months.

'I'll need to take on another man, Tam – not a horseman, mind, just a labourer. You'll still be Boss and the others can come to you for their instructions.

'Oh, and I'm thinking of getting a woman in to look after you.'

Angus stopped there because he could see that Tam was tiring and anyway he was not yet ready to tell him everything. There was still so much to arrange.

But it could be done. It would be done. It *had* to be done.

'Right, Tam, you get some sleep – and stop worrying. I hired you to make my horses the best known on the East Coast. And that's exactly what's going to happen. We just need a wee bit more time.'

And a lot of luck, he added to himself grimly.

Ruby stood at the window rocking wee Ishbel in her arms. 'You just don't understand what's happening, my wee lambie,' Ruby whispered, 'and your mammy hasnae time for you the day.

'But I have time,' she crooned. 'I'll always have time for you.'

She picked up the woollen shawl from the bed and wrapped it round the baby. 'There you are, my darlin'. You're like a wee clootie dumplin' ready to be boiled.'

She carried the baby downstairs, but instead of going down the uncarpeted back stairs, she went to the front of the house and into Matron's sitting-room.

There were four people in the room, Matron, Hazel the maid, the minister who came every Sunday afternoon, and a fine, tall, good-looking young man, at whom Ruby smiled coyly.

'She's jist coming,' she said and then she laughed coarsely. 'Did the blushing bride no' have to feed her bairn first? There's a richt turn-up – a bride wi' a bairn!'

'Sit down and be quiet!' Matron ordered. 'Or you and the baby can go straight back upstairs.'

Ruby sat down instantly. Soon, too soon, wee Ishbel was going to be taken from her and so she treasured every moment she had with the precious baby.

Rowena had promised that she could still see the child occasionally and she prayed that she would keep her word.

'I want tae see this wedding, Matron,' she said. 'A handsome 'groom.' Again she smiled her hideous, coy smile. 'And a beautiful bride.'

The door opened then and Rowena came in. She was wearing a pale grey silk dress and her crystal earrings sparkled in the light.

157

Her magnificent black hair was tied back with pale yellow ribbons and she looked devastatingly lovely.

She looked first at Ruby to reassure herself that all was well with her baby and only then did she look at the two men.

'Dear God, but you're beautiful, really beautiful,' Matt exclaimed, as she walked over to stand beside him.

The minister frowned at the improper use of the Lord's name.

'Please,' he said, 'I'd like to get this ceremony over quickly.'

'It's a wedding,' Matt reminded him. 'A joyous occasion.'

The minister flushed. He didn't like to be corrected, so he decided to punish Matt by leaving out the words 'Dearly Beloved.'

And at the very moment that Rowena MacFarlane married Matthew Grey, a convoy of caravans – a yellow one missing – arrived in Forfarshire…

The earth under the trees was brightly starred with primroses.

Spotting them, Rowena smiled and bent down so that wee Ishbel could see them, too.

The baby yawned, showing perfect little

pink gums. As yet, she had no interest whatsoever in the natural beauties of the world around her.

Her mother interested her, though, and sometimes the other person with the deep voice, who lifted her high, high into the air...

Rowena picked a few of the tiny flowers. It was a silly thing to do. They'd wilt quickly. She should have waited until she was walking home again. *Home* ... there was a wonderful word.

They were waiting for her, as she had known they would be. The dogs would have warned of her coming.

He came to meet her.

So much had happened to her, but he was unchanged. Or was he?

She had to stop her hand from straying up to touch the side of his face, where a few grey hairs were showing against the blue black. And the eyes, too? What had happened to take the light out of his eyes?

'My mother is gone,' he said, answering her unspoken question. He had always seemed to know what she was thinking. 'It was an accident, a tragic accident. Yet I feel so responsible. Maybe if I had...'

'Oh, Marek,' she interrupted, squeezing his hand gently. That tiny gesture expressed all her compassion and reassurance. No more needed to be said.

'Thanks, Rowena.' He smiled tenderly. 'Right, come and have some tea and show us our new baby sister. What's she called?'

'Ishbel,' she replied softly. 'I named her for your mother.'

Visibly moved by her words, he took the baby from her and with gentle hands lifted the shawl from Ishbel's face. Round, dark, little eyes gazed solemnly into his.

'She smiled at me!'

'It was wind,' the doting mother replied, chuckling brightly.

She took the baby from him and they strolled back to the gypsy encampment.

When they arrived, they sat down on a log by the fire.

'We'd like some tea,' Marek said to Pheemie Stewart, his partner.

Roughly, the woman poured hot tea into a tin mug, but it was with careful hands that she handed it to the new mother.

She may bitterly resent the fact that Marek still carried a torch for Rowena, but Pheemie would do nothing to harm her or the infant she was nursing.

'I've put two sugars in and some good, fresh milk – for the bairn, see.'

Rowena smiled up at her, but Pheemie just glared back at her.

Confused, Rowena looked at Marek.

'She thinks you're a rival,' he explained.

'Me? Oh, that's silly. Maybe once, long

ago, Marek, but no more. I have a man now and wee Ishbel has a father. We even have a cottage of our own. I'll do nothing to spoil all that. Matt loves us.'

'And Ishbel's real father?'

'You have no right to ask about him.'

'Maybe not – but I have the right of a true friend to worry about you.' He poured more tea and changed the subject.

'I hear this Matt of yours is an educated man who's pretending that he's a farm labourer.'

Rowena sipped her scaldingly-hot tea. It never seemed to get as hot as this at the farm.

Poor Matt... She would not tell Marek that he almost stumbled over the door night after night, exhausted from the hard, manual labour to which he was completely unaccustomed.

Angus Campbell had given him a home and a job, but, in return, he expected his new employee to do the work properly – and, to his credit, Matt was trying.

'He has brains and he's willing to learn, Marek. In a few months' time, Tam Laird's coming to bide with us.

'That was one of Mister Campbell's main conditions when he took Matt and I on. I'll look after Tam while he's getting better and we'll all share the cottage.'

'A two-roomed cottage for four folk and

maybe some more bairns to come? That's difficult enough when you're all kin, Rowena…'

'We'll worry about that when the time comes.' There was no need to tell him that she was not living with Matt as husband and wife. They slept in separate beds, so there was no prospect of 'more bairns'.

Matt was a gentleman who'd given his word not to touch her, and although Marek would understand the honour of that, he'd still think that Matt was a fool. Fancy having a beautiful wife like Rowena and agreeing not to go near her…

'I'd best get back,' Rowena said then. 'Mistress Campbell may send for me. She'll want blood for her bargain that one, and I hear she's not too pleased about me being back on her land. I think it's only the fact that Matt's the minister's son that stills her tongue.'

They stood up and he put his strong, muscular arms round her and the baby. 'Damn these gorgios and their narrow ways, Rowena! Here, you'd be queen and everyone would acknowledge your position.

'Come away with us and raise the baby among your own folk, where she belongs.'

'I've promised myself to Matt, as he has to me, Marek. You wouldn't expect me to break my vows, would you?'

'No, but I'd expect to hear you speak of

love, Rowena,' he said. 'I haven't yet…'

'He's a good man – it'll come.'

'And I'm a good man, too, am I not, Rowena MacFarlane? The difference is, I'm ready to love you now – and for all time.'

Gently, she disentangled herself from his embrace. 'It's Rowena Grey now, Marek,' she said softly.

'For all time,' he repeated, but if she heard him, she paid no heed.

Lizzie Campbell watched Rowena walk past the farmhouse, her baby cradled in her arms, and her head held high.

Like a queen, Lizzie fumed inwardly. *She walks like a queen!*

Oh, Angus Campbell, you'll suffer for bringing that woman back on to my farm!

Indeed, he'd begun to suffer already…

'I can't believe you hired that woman again!' she'd raged when she'd first heard. 'Not after all I said.'

'I never hired her,' Angus had replied truthfully. How many times had he mentally gone over what he would say to Lizzie, how he would explain? 'I hired Matt Grey – and that was a bit of a masterstroke.'

He'd realised he had to get her as charged with enthusiasm about Matt's appointment as he was himself.

'Look, Lizzie, the boy's a wizard wi' figures and writes a neat hand. He'll be a tremendous help with the business side of things and his ... his, em, wife will take care of Tam Laird.

'I couldn't afford to lose Tam, lass. *We* couldn't. The thing is, he has no kin.

'It would be the workhouse for him if the hospital discharged him now. He's simply not fit for work yet and I wouldn't dream of asking you to take him in here.

'He'll need a lot of careful nursing for months yet...'

She had bridled. 'Are you saying I'm not capable of looking after him?'

'Ach, Lizzie, if I was ill, it would be your sweet face I'd want smiling down at me. So would any man.

'But you have two wee lads underfoot all the time, and you've me and the house to look after. Besides, you're not strongly built like ... Mistress Grey.'

He had thought for a moment, then he'd added, 'And there's the connection with the Manse, of course. The minister and his wife will be visiting here regularly. That'll please your mother ... you and Mrs Walter Grey calling on one another socially.'

Lizzie had considered this. Yes, her mother would be pleased.

'Well, I'll still need someone else to help me in the house. As for that gypsy trollop, well, I suppose it'll be all right... But, Angus, are you sure Tam *will* get well again?'

She'd seen a look of real distaste and disappointment cross his face.

'Do I sound cold, Angus? Don't get me wrong – I like Tam – we all do. But my father always said a farmer couldn't afford to be sentimental.'

His stern, unyielding expression had had her quickly backtracking.

'I'm not saying we'd abandon Tam. Not at all. Goodness, with the new century almost on us, those bad old days are gone. But we do have two children to feed, Angus...'

Children? That had opened a new train of thought.

Matt Grey couldn't possibly be Rowena's baby's father, Lizzie had mused. He just couldn't be.

'How on earth did that woman get her hooks into poor Matthew? He definitely wasn't born to farm work. He's a gentleman, Angus.'

And damned glad of a job and a roof over his head, Angus had thought – but he hadn't said it.

'I think he did all the running, lass. She's a bonny woman, if you like the, well, gypsy look.

'Anyway, what does it matter? It's worked out well for us, that's the main thing.'

'Matt needed a job and the minister's son couldn't go in the bothy with the halflins, could he? It just wouldn't be right. Besides, his father is now grateful to us, Lizzie, *very* grateful.'

A sudden, terrifying thought had struck Lizzie then, but she hadn't been able to voice it: she never would. If she did, her marriage would be over.

'I've never been happy with the interest you took in that tinker, Angus. You're soft and women like her take advantage. Ay, and there's talk...

'All the neighbours are wondering why she's back so soon when she left in disgrace.'

Angus had blustered. 'Well, I could hardly tell Matt Grey that he could work here, but his wife wasn't welcome. Anyway, we don't have to have anything to do with her, Lizzie.'

He'd known what to say to cause her concern; how to give her something else to worry about, besides the name of the new bairn's father...

'You'd best keep a close eye on our two lads. I've seen both of them down at that cottage this past week, you know.'

'Well, I can't be everywhere! *You* tell them to stay away from that woman.' She'd still seemed puzzled, though.

'Angus, how did Matt Grey ever meet her?' she'd asked. 'He *can't* be that bairn's father! What his poor mother must be going through, I can't bear to think.'

She had wanted to ask him. She had even

166

felt the words of the big question forming on the tip of her tongue.

She had decided to ask outright and these awful suspicions would at least be aired at last. She *had* to know. She just had to find out.

But her courage had failed her at the eleventh hour and she had compromised.

'Angus,' she had asked, quietly, 'do you know who the child's father is?'

He had not lied, but he hadn't told the truth either – and, fortunately, she had accepted his answer without rancour.

'Lizzie, what secrets lie between Matt Grey and his lawfully-wedded wife are none of our business,' he'd told her. 'We'll just conduct ourselves like good Christians. You need never clap eyes on Rowena again. All right?'

'And what if Mrs Grey calls round expecting to see her daughter-in-law? How will I avoid seeing the damned tinker then?' Lizzie's anger had risen again and so had her hatred of Rowena MacFarlane.

Angus had taken refuge in work at that point. He'd rammed his bunnet on the back of his head and walked briskly to the door. 'If she wants to see Rowena, I expect she'll go round to her son's house!'

His patience had finally snapped. 'Right, I've had enough of this – and I've horses to tend to. I'll be back when you can find something else to talk about!'

He had somehow managed not to slam the door as he'd gone out, head bent, into the driving rain...

Mrs Walter Grey had no intention of visiting the woman her son had married. Indeed, she had taken to her bed when the news of the marriage had reached her – and had stayed there for an extra few days when details of her son's new job were explained to her.

'Chrissie, my dear. I know it's not what we wanted for Matthew,' her husband consoled later when he visited her in her 'sickbed'. He knelt down beside her.

Chrissie sobbed loudly and turned her head away. 'You did this, Walter Grey? You did this! Imagine, my son, my Matt, and that tinker woman. The local gossips'll have a field day! They'll say it's his child.'

Swiftly, she turned to face him again. 'Right, you'll just have to apply for another job. We can't stay here with the entire parish laughing at us.'

'If they're laughing, then we probably deserve their ridicule, Chrissie.' He tried to take her in his arms. 'But folk are better than you think, my dear.

'No-one seriously believes that Matt's the child's father. They think he's a dreamer and a soppy, romantic fool, but most of them wish him well.

'"*Never thought he had it in him,*" the Session Clerk told me today and that was a compliment. They're impressed that Matt's found a job – and stuck to it. Of course, it's not what we wanted for him, or what he was brought up to consider, but at least it's honest toil and, as I say, he's sticking to it.'

'Two weeks is hardly "sticking to it"!' She sobbed.

Walter got up from his undignified position beside the bed and went to the window. His wife would not be consoled. They would just have to work through this crisis. Once she was over the initial shock, she would realise that they must be seen to accept the marriage.

The grey, damp weather outside echoed his wife's misery.

'In an hour or two, there'll be a rainbow, Chrissie. Maybe you'll feel well enough to get up to see it, dear. And then we must go to Matt's new home and take a housewarming gift. My mother's porcelain teapot would be appropriate, I think.

'And then, of course, they must visit us here. I'll christen the baby in the church … this Sunday afternoon, don't you think?

'We must put on a brave front. We'll need a Christening cake, dear, and some scones.'

'Right, I suppose I'll have to get that organised,' she said, without much enthusiasm. 'You know I'll do my Christian duty, Walter, but I'll never love that hussy.'

He said nothing. If that spiteful barb made her feel better for a little, then so be it.

But he knew that if Rowena MacFarlane made her son happy – and Walter was sure she would – the new Mrs Grey would eventually find no better friend than her reluctant mother-in-law…

Matt Grey decided that it was all the small, detestable things that made life miserable. He'd learned to deal with major calamities, like having no home and no money. That was simple.

You just took any job that was offered to raise some cash. He did not object to hard labour, even when it was dirty and smelly like his current task – mucking out the byres at Springhill.

But the small things, like rain squirming down the back of his neck so that he was getting wet from both the inside and the outside at the same time – that, he found almost unbearable. And thick, claggy mud oozing over the top of his work boots – he loathed that, too.

He stood up to stretch his back and for no apparent reason found himself thinking back to the decadence of that last excessive Christmas party at the Windmill Bar in Dundee.

He could practically feel the heat from the fire, taste the mulled wine and smell the fruit in the punch. In his memory, he lay back in a luxurious armchair and stretched his long legs to the warmth of the fire…

'Having a wee break, lad, or are you expecting the muck tae lift itsel' aff the ground?'

It was the grieve and if he expected a quick pulling of the forelock and a muttered apology from Matt, he was disappointed.

Instead, Matt chuckled good-humouredly. 'More wishing than expecting, gaffer,' he said and began to dig again and lift, dig and lift. 'It'd make a heck of a difference to my back, if the stuff did fly into the barrow all by itself!'

The grieve watched him for a while. He heard no insolence in the remark. It had been said with great humour. He shook his head and left the byre.

If he had been raised a son of the Manse, he doubted if he would be able to find laughter in a midden.

Ay, the gentry were strange folk and Matt Grey was definitely gentry, even if he was up to his knees in muck.

Matt worked on, his screaming muscles begging him to stop – and at last the job was finally done. Unfortunately for him, though, there was another chore, just as dirty, just as necessary, to follow.

Well, I asked for this job, Matt told himself, and I know everyone is expecting me to fail. Maybe that's why I'm trying so hard.

What am I doing working as a labourer, though? Proving to my father that I'm not totally useless, or trying to humiliate him before his parishioners?

No, I wouldn't want to upset my parents ... to be honest, I never even thought about how this would affect them. When have I ever?

But I'll not fail this time. I'll earn their respect – and Rowena's...

He sighed at the thought of his wife; his beautiful wife, who cooked his meals and who uncomplainingly washed his filthy clothes – and who slept alone in the big double bed in the back room...

At last the gaffer released the men from their misery. All of them knew that if this spring rain did not let up, there would be more misery waiting for them tomorrow and the day after.

Matt wiped his shovels clean with old hay and hung them on a nail to dry in a warm corner of the barn. Woe betide anyone who let their tools rust.

Now he was free to walk home. With a parting joke, he left the halflins – the young apprentices – who were off to share a meal in the Bothy and walked on down the lane to where the old cottage stood.

Smoke was rising in a clean plume from the newly-swept chimneys and his spirits rose with the smoke. It would be warm in there, and Rowena would have hot soup ready and water for him to wash off all the muck of the day, boiling on the back of the fire.

Matt arrived at the gate and felt a momentary thrill. This gate opened on to the path that led to the door of *his own home*.

When he peered through the window, he saw that there was a lamp on in the front room and its gentle glow lit the farthest corner, where the firelight did not reach.

Rowena was sitting in her chair by the flickering fire. In her hands, were the makings of a rag rug.

One foot was gently rocking the cradle where Ishbel lay. The dancing flames and the lamplight picked out gold highlights in his wife's black hair.

At the sight of her, Matt's heart contracted in his chest. How beautiful she was, yet seemingly so unaware of it.

His wife, his wife. What lovely words – but she was not really his wife... Oh, how he yearned to touch her, to hold her, to bury his face in her glorious hair.

If only she knew how many times he had longed to pull her into his arms...

She bent to the baby and he saw her hair fall across her beautiful profile. She was breathtaking. Where had all that beauty come from, that strength of character, that infectious sense of humour?

Then he moved and his sudden shadow startled her and she looked up.

She stared at him quietly through the window for a moment, then smiled and moved gracefully to open the door.

'Come away in, you daft gowk! You must be freezing out there.'

He allowed himself to be pulled into the room. When the door was closed behind him, he blurted out the words, 'You really are a lovely woman, Rowena.'

He hadn't meant to say anything provocative like that. He would never force himself on any woman. Despite his colourful past, that was his code and he would stick by it.

If his words had shocked her, there was no evidence of it. She simply held his gaze and said, 'And you're a lovely man, Matt Grey.' Then, awkwardly, she added, 'But you'll be a sick one if you don't get over to that fire and warm yourself up!'

She helped him off with his wet jacket and boots and he watched her stuff the footwear with paper and hang the coat where the heat from the fire could reach it.

He tiptoed past the cradle to the table,

stopping to glance in as he passed.

'How old will Ishbel have to be before she's awake to see her daddy coming home from work?'

For a moment, he thought she had misinterpreted his question. He wasn't the child's real father after all.

But then Rowena laughed. 'Oh, she'll be under your feet in no time at all. Then you'll be complaining about her being a wee nuisance. Just wait...'

She put a bowl with hot mutton stew on the table and then, to his delight, prepared another bowl for herself and sat down across from him.

Every other night of their unusual, two-week marriage, she had eaten before he'd come limping home.

Matt reached for the bread, then politely held it out first to Rowena.

As he watched her eat, Matt once again felt his heart behaving in the strangest fashion. Then his hands began to shake.

How embarrassing, he thought. *I'm trembling like a lovesick boy...*

He bent his head to concentrate on his meal and said no more until he had finished every savoury morsel. When he'd done so, Rowena was instantly by his side to refill his bowl.

He said nothing, just clasped his hands together tightly, because the longing to touch her as she passed was intense and he was terrified of making a wrong move.

But she's your wife. She's your wife. Then he remembered what he'd promised her as they'd walked away from the Refuge. *'I love you, Rowena,'* he'd told her. *'I can't sleep for thinking of you, but I'll not touch you unless you give me leave. I mean that.'*

Now, they finished their meal in silence, but it was companionable rather than awkward. Matt was exhausted and Rowena, too, was tired from her day's work.

The fire occasionally spat and sizzled behind them and from the cradle came endearing little murmurs as the baby slept on, dreaming of warm milk and loving arms.

And when the stew was finished and the last gravy had been mopped up by chunks of Rowena's home-baked bread, she stood up and held out her hand to the tired man at the table.

'Come, husband,' she said softly and there was infinite promise in her voice and her eyes. 'It's time you were warm in bed.'

And he took her hand and went with her, not into the little room at the back, but into the bigger room at the front, where, for the last two weeks, Rowena had slept alone.

Now she closed the door softly behind them and turned naturally into Matt's waiting arms...

The whole world was going to the Feein'
Market in Forfar...

It had been a long, cold winter and a wet
spring. Then there had been Tam's accident,
which had lowered the spirits of everyone in
the close-knit community.

Now it was time for fun.

'The Boss is taking us all to the market –
and he's paying!' The halflins were as excited
as 15-year-olds have every right to be. Their
childhood, if they had ever had one, had
ended years ago.

Now they were doing a man's job, day in,
day out, and they had little to show for their
efforts at the end of the quarter. The Boss
taking them to the fair in his cart was a real
treat and their high spirits infected everyone.

'You go with the Maister and his two
sons,' Rowena encouraged Matt. 'You
deserve a break and if I don't have to make
a meal for you, I can have a good day
cleaning out the wee room for Tam.

'I want it nice for him. A fresh coat of
whitewash and a rag rug on the floor and
he'll be as comfortable as the Laird in his
big hoose!'

Matt hugged her to him and she returned
his kisses, laughing merrily. 'Away you go
afore you wake the bairn and I make you
take her to the market an' all!'

Matt chuckled, dropped a soft kiss on Ishbel's pearly little forehead and then almost ran to the steading. He was a happy man. His father was his friend again. His wife was the best of women, truly the best.

And his job … well, to be honest, he hated it, but at least it was honest toil, which allowed him to put a roof over his family and food on their table.

Now he was off to watch the jugglers at the Feein' Market, to buy a velvet ribbon for Rowena and a doll for his wee princess, his Ishbel.

He had saved the money secretly since he'd heard that Angus Campbell was taking them all to the Feein' Market. He'd buy green velvet ribbons for Rowena – and, oh, the joy of her tender reward.

They all sang happily as the cart trundled through the country lanes and out on to the road, where it soon ran into a veritable convoy of other like-minded country folk.

Angus's two boys, Colin and James, scrambled between their father and Matt, seeking news of the baby, whom sometimes, when their mother was busy, they ran down to the cottage to see.

They would have liked Ishbel to live in their house and often asked if they could have a baby of their own. They never got a proper answer to their request, though…

At the fairground, Matt went off on his

own. He had his reasons for not spending extra time in the company of his employer.

He resented the fact that this self-styled 'pillar of society' was the father of his Rowena's child. He detested the way Angus had crumbled so easily to his blackmail, and had given Matt a job...

Besides, there would be recruiting sergeants at the Market and he would enjoy their banter.

'Matthew Grey, as I live and breathe! Good to see you again, lad...'

The huge sergeant who guarded the front of the biggest ale wagon, greeted Matt like a long-lost brother and for some time Matt enjoyed the camaraderie and the atmosphere of military life.

'Will you take Her Majesty's shilling this time, Matt?'

''Fraid not. It's too late, my friend. I have a bonny wife and a baby at home waiting for me with open arms. Actually, I'm only here to buy fairings for my own fair ones.'

'Well, I hope you'll have a glass or two with me later, Matt, for old times' sake.'

'I will indeed – but later. I know you, Donald. A bucketful of drink, a few hands of cards and I'd be going home with empty pockets and a sore head!'

They laughed, understanding one another well. Heartened by the meeting, Matt went off to enjoy the fun of the fair. He tried his hand at arm-wrestling with 'The World's Strongest Man', but he was not strong enough!

Then he attempted to shoot at a tiny bullseye on a target, but he had not been bred to the gun and it was Angus who won the prize rag doll, which he tried to press on Matt for Ishbel.

'No thank you. I'll buy my bairn's toy myself, Master,' Matt said with audible contempt in his voice and Angus flushed and turned away.

He knows – of course he knows. I should never forget that, Angus reminded himself. *I wonder if he and Rowena talk about me? No, somehow I can't believe that he's asked her about me.*

He just wants me to remember that I'm the bairn's father and that he'll use the information when and where it suits him.

Without thinking, Angus thrust the doll into young Jamie's arms.

'I'm far too big for daft wee dollies, Daddy!' Jamie protested, throwing the embarrassing object into the mud. 'Anyway, they're for lassies,' he added contemptuously.

As if to prove his point, a ragged little girl from another farm snatched up the doll and rushed off with it, her delight in her good fortune tinged with guilt and fear of being reprimanded.

Matt, his good humour gone, pushed the fairings he had bought inside his jacket and set off to walk home. It would be a long, tiring hike but, thank goodness, Rowena would be there at the end of it.

He imagined her long black hair spilling down as he released it from its pins, just so that he could tie it up again in his bright green ribbons, and his steps and his breathing grew faster.

He wished he had bought a bacon piece – a sandwich – or a Forfar bridie to ease his hunger, but there would be soup at the back of the fire and fresh, crusty bread.

'Meat for a king!' he said out loud, smiling to himself.

Matthew breasted the top of a hill and looked down on to the valley spread out before him. He looked into the distance.

Could he see a plume of smoke from his own chimney? No, of course not! He dismissed that stupid thought with a laugh and tramped on.

That was when he thought he saw a horse and rider on the road below him.

It was late afternoon, but darkness was hours away yet and he was not too concerned. Still, he looked around for a sturdy stick he could use as a weapon should the need arise.

Yes, there *was* a horse, and on it was a man – a man who stared at him with dark eyes that looked vaguely familiar and were filled with hate.

In his hand, the man carried a shotgun, which he lifted menacingly so that the barrel was pointing straight at Matt.

Matt threw down his stick. What use was it against an armed man?

'What the hell's going on? What do you want?' he asked, trying not to sound afraid. 'Listen, I'm just a farm labourer. There's nothing in my pockets but fairings for my wife and baby.'

'What I want from you is not in your pocket, Gorgio! Let me introduce myself. My name is Marek, Marek MacFarlane.'

Rowena put baby Ishbel safely in the centre of the big bed and went back into the kitchen for the brightly-coloured rag rug she had just finished making. It was just what was needed to make the room a bit cheerier for Tam Laird's forthcoming arrival from hospital.

Matt had laughed at her when she'd mentioned her concern.

'Sweetheart–' how easily that term of endearment slipped from his lips these days '–Tam's spent his whole life in bothies! This is real luxury compared with that!'

But Rowena looked around the small bedroom now and sighed. It was so bare and cold.

At least the reds and oranges, the yellows and browns in the rug made the room look warmer.

'I'll do a bed cover next, eh, Ishbel?' she said to her baby, who was gurgling happily, waving her fat little legs in the air.

'Weena!' a shrill voice called from the next room and Rowena lifted her daughter and hurried into the kitchen.

'Hello, my wee lambs,' she greeted her two visitors warmly.

James and Colin Campbell were standing in the open doorway of the cottage.

They had opened the door, but had waited politely for permission to enter.

'Come in, lads. Come ben.'

'We've brought a lucky horseshoe for Tam,' Colin told her, as he pushed his little brother into the room. 'Daddy says it's one of Fern's.'

'It's a present, Weena,' Jamie added unnecessarily.

Still with wee Ishbel in her arms, Rowena hugged each of the little boys.

'That's smashin', lads. Terrific! And don't I know the very place for it! Here Colin, you hold Ishbel – very carefully, mind – while Jamie and I fix this.

'It's one of Fern's shoes, did you say?

183

Tam'll love that. He was that fond of the mare. What a pity...' Rowena stopped there, not wanting to dwell on the tragic accident that had hospitalised Springhill's senior horseman.

'Right, where'll we put it?' she asked, changing the subject.

Jamie wanted the horseshoe to hang above Tam's bed.

'You're daft! It'll hit his head gin it falls!' Colin pointed out scornfully.

'Ay, but Jamie has a point, Colin,' Rowena said, intervening quickly. 'It's just the thing for him to see while he's lying in his bed.

'But, for safety's sake, I think we'll put it on the other wall. All right?'

And after the horseshoe had been hung in the best spot, Rowena took the children into the kitchen, where Jamie could be seated in a deep chair, so that he, too, could have a turn at holding the baby.

Rowena was only too aware that the boys should not be at her cottage; their mother – and possibly their father, too – certainly didn't want the sons of the farm to fraternise with Rowena Grey's baby, but she could not bring herself to deny them.

They loved running in for a few minutes to look at the baby quietly if Ishbel was asleep, or to hold her if she was awake.

'Maybe now Jamie's had a wee shot of holding Ishbel, you should be getting back, boys,' she began, but Colin smiled at her reassuringly.

'Don't worry, Rowena. Daddy sent us down here with the horseshoe and he said he'd collect us on his way up to the house.'

Angus coming here! Coming to this house! Rowena did not know what to think. Confused feelings rushed through her.

She had not spoken to Angus since the day she and Matt had arrived at the farm after their wedding and that had been a very stilted conversation.

'Welcome to Springhill Farm, Matt,' Angus had said formally. Then he had turned to her. 'I hope you'll both be very happy here, Mrs Grey.'

It was the first time she had ever been called Mrs Grey and the fact that it was Angus who had said the words made them poignant somehow...

He had avoided looking at the babe in her arms and she, naturally, had made no effort to bring wee Ishbel to his attention.

But now he had deliberately given himself an opportunity to talk to her, to see the baby – his baby – even though his sons would also be in the house.

'Right then, if your daddy's coming for you, we'll have time for milk and gingerbread!' she said as lightly as she could. 'Do you remember my gingerbread? Well, Matt loves it almost as much as you two. I'm

185

forever baking it!'

Their father knocked at the door just as the boys were finishing their snack, and, for the first time in weeks, Rowena and Angus were face to face.

His glance met hers for less than a moment and then he looked at Jamie.

'Well, I hope these two have behaved themselves. I'll take them off your hands now, Mistress,' he said, but he was looking at Ishbel as he spoke.

Angus remembered the joy he had experienced when he'd first seen Colin and then wee Jamie, but he was unprepared for the feeling that flooded through him now as he looked at the baby cradled in his small son's arms.

My only daughter, he acknowledged silently to his innermost heart, as the big eyes looked unblinkingly into his.

'Isn't she the beautifullest baby you ever saw, Daddy?' Jamie remarked innocently.

'She's a lot better than Jamie was, Daddy,' Colin said, turning to Rowena. 'Do you remember, Rowena? Jamie girned all the time.'

'I did not! I hardly cried at all!' Jamie responded angrily and the baby slipped in his arms.

Automatically, Angus reached for her and lifted her expertly into his arms.

Again, deep emotion throbbed in his veins

as he held the small, warm infant. He looked at Rowena and his eyes were filled with unspoken questions and promises.

'She's so bonny, so very bonny,' was all he said.

Rowena looked gravely back at the father of her child. She could see the love in his eyes, not for her but for his daughter. She saw his hopes, his genuine commitment. He had meant what he said.

Ishbel was Angus's child, just as Colin and Jamie were and, one day, Ishbel Grey would have a share in this farm.

'All babies are lovely,' Rowena said lightly, as she took the child from him.

But her eyes said, *I realise how deeply you care for her, so don't worry, I'll never take her away from here. This is where she belongs.*

'I've got a letter here from the Dundee infirmary, Lizzie,' Angus Campbell remarked to his wife, one late summer evening.

'It says Tam can be discharged, but we'll have to collect him, because he still can't walk more than a step or two. Could you take the trap...?'

Lizzie was shocked. 'Me? Drive the trap into Dundee to pick up one of the workmen! Right in the middle of the harvest, too, when I do nothing but cook and wash up and bake for the workers!

And I haven't even mentioned the house or the hens or your two boys. Remember them?

'Ay,' she went on sarcastically, 'don't you worry yourself. I'll just put on my best hat and take myself off to Dundee for the day. Maybe I'll even have time for lunch at Lamb's Corner House!'

Your two boys. They were always *his* boys when she was displeased. He held up his hands, suitably admonished.

'All right, all right! I just thought you might enjoy a wee break, dear. Don't worry, though. I'll get Matt Grey to go.

'He's getting really good with a horse and cart, you know. Maybe giving him a chance to chat away to Tam on his own is not a bad idea.'

Matt was pleased to be trusted with one of Tam Laird's beloved horses. He encouraged the older man to lean on him, while Tam walked unsteadily from the door of the hospital to the cart, where Gavin's Boy stood like a rock in the shafts.

The great Clydesdale's ears twitched as he heard their approach and then he uttered a whinny of recognition.

Tam leaned his head against the horse. 'Ah, you beautiful big fella,' he crooned.

Matt half lifted Tam into the cart and tried to wrap a blanket round his legs.

'Away, I dinna need that on a grand day like this, lad! I'm fine now – the smell of a horse is the best medicine for a man like me.'

They headed home slowly, Matt understandably nervous about daring to drive the first horseman; Tam savouring the knowledge that he was, indeed, going to recover among his beautiful horses.

The fields were busy as they reached the farm. The hairst, the harvest, was in full swing and the warm smell of freshly-cut hay drifted across to them.

'I swear I can even smell the briar roses, Matt lad!' Tam quipped, then chuckled as the dust caused Matt to sneeze mightily.

'You're no' a born farmer, laddie, but stick with us. I've heard nothin' but good about you. They say you're no' bad wi' the horses.'

Matt blew his nose and laughed good naturedly.

'Well, I'm working at it, Tam, but sometimes it's slow. Right, I'll take you home now. My wife's waiting to give you the best meal you've had in months.'

Tam laid a work-worn hand on Matt's arm. 'I'm going to be a nuisance to Mistress Grey for weeks to come, lad. I know that, but could I ask one more favour and risk annoying her further? Do you think I could see Fern's foal afore we go home?'

'Well, if you promise not to notice how

189

clumsily I turn Gavin's Boy around, Tam, I'll take you anywhere you want to go!'

After a couple of false starts, Matt turned the cart and they ambled slowly off to the field where the foal was spending most of the summer.

She was not alone. An elderly mare occupied the field with her.

'We just thought the company would be good for her, Tam – but look at what's happened.'

Tam said nothing, but his face told Matt everything he wanted to know. Tears glistened in the horseman's eyes as he watched the foal play in the field beside her foster mother.

When she began to butt at the mare's flanks and then suckle, tears slipped slowly down Tam's weathered cheeks.

'I've heard tell of this but I've never actually seen it, lad,' he whispered hoarsely. 'She's treating the wee filly as her own. That's fantastic!'

'Well, it was wee Colin's idea to put them together. You'll be proud of that laddie, Tam. In his innocence, he said that old Betsy could be the foal's mother and he was the only one of us who wasn't surprised when her milk did come in.'

'It's high time the foal had a name,' Tam said gruffly, to cover the shame of his tears. 'It'll hae to be something that'll remind us of her mother.

'Now, let's get moving, lad. Your missus is waiting and I wouldn't want to get off to a bad start.'

Matt protested that everything would be fine, but drove steadily to the little cottage.

Rowena had been watching for them and Tam's first glimpse of her nearly took his breath away. She was so beautiful.

She was standing in the doorway under an arch of white and yellow rambling roses, the heady perfume of which blew to him across the garden.

Ye daft gowk, Tam Laird! he silently chided himself. To think you were offered all that and you turned it down! Well, she's got a good man in young Matt, nae matter who her bairn's faither is.

'Good day to you, Mistress Grey,' he said formally. 'I hope I won't be too much of a burden.'

Rowena reached up a strong hand to help him from the cart.

'Hello, Tam,' she replied. 'Welcome to your own home. And you can forget all that "burden" nonsense! Anything we can do for you, we'll do gladly.'

She smiled at Matt and Tam saw the softness in her eyes.

'There'll be soup on the table, Matt, as soon as you're ready for it,' she said.

She helped Tam into the kitchen and

settled him in the big chair beside the fireplace, where a beautiful arrangement of dried beech leaves hid the empty grate.

The baby was in her cradle, but she was wide awake and the first Tam saw of her was plump healthy little limbs waving in the air.

'A horseman's legs!' Tam announced fondly and with three words became a valued member of the family.

The hairst was a good one and Angus went to bed at night aware of the grain filling his barns, of the shillings that would soon swell his bank account – and of the fact that Tam Laird was once more asleep at Springhill Farm.

August and September were happy months for Angus and would have been glorious were it not for his wife's growing discontent.

At the beginning of September, Lizzie sent a tear-stained note to her mother and, soon after, Angus drove to the station to fetch his mother-in-law, Mrs Watson.

'Lizzie's never been strong, Angus. Didn't her father and I tell you that the day you were wed? Here she is with no inside help and expected to do the work of two women.

'Then she's supposed to be the perfect hostess if the minister's wife comes to call.

'It's too much. You hired that tinker girl to help and here poor Lizzie is, not two years later, with more work to do than ever. You'll need to find a skivvy for her. You'll *have* to!'

'I'll see what I can do,' Angus promised in the hope that Lizzie's mother would not ask awkward questions about the hasty dismissal of Rowena MacFarlane.

'Maybe I'll see somebody at the next Feein' Market.'

'No! Put an advertisement in the *Courier and Journal*, Angus – NOW! – and get Lizzie some good, hardworking help...'

Finally spurred into action, Angus dropped Mrs Watson off at the house and went straight back to Dundee to the newspaper office.

It was a lovely afternoon and for a moment he wished he had picked up his boys, but no doubt they would prefer to stay at home to see what surprises Granny had hidden in her suitcase.

He turned off the Perth Road and suddenly thought of the Women's Refuge. Yes, perhaps he could find a suitable woman there!

Someone clean, conscientious, honest and hardworking – that's what he was after.

He was offered Ruby Dunbar.

'She's no oil painting,' the Matron admitted, 'and she has been the wrong side of the law once or twice. Quite often, actually – but it's circumstances that drive women like Ruby to sin, Mr Campbell.

'Her husband should have been locked up for what he did to her, but to the authorities a woman's no more than a man's possession – more's the pity. For all that, she's spotlessly clean, and a real hard worker.'

She did not add that she would be delighted to get Ruby off her hands, especially since MacFarlane had married and left them. Somehow, the vital spark of Ruby had gone with Rowena.

Nowadays, the pale, silent creature who flitted like a ghost up and down the stairs was no match for the louder, stronger element among the residents.

She'd have sorted any of them out a few months ago, Matron thought to herself. *Can't think what ails her. And if she's caught some kind of illness, I want her out of here – quickly!*

Meantime, Angus was caught up in his own thoughts. He was imagining going back to the farm with a maid-of-all-work in tow, and seeing Lizzie smiling and his mother-in-law looking on him with approval – and the very idea made him forget his exhaustion.

He had been working since daybreak and was tired and hungry, but if Lizzie was happy…

'I'll take her,' he said firmly.

Matron smiled. 'It's not that simple, Mr Campbell. I'm afraid Dunbar will have to be consulted. She's quite likely to storm out of

194

here and do something stupid if she feels she's being coerced.'

And then I'll get her back when the police have finished with her, she thought – but naturally she didn't say anything.

Ruby was eventually summoned. She did not know Angus and stared at him fearfully.

'Mr Campbell has come to offer you a living-in position, Ruby. You'd be a maid in a nice house on a farm. It's not a big family – there's just Mr and Mrs Campbell and their two nice wee boys.

'I hear they're both as good as gold and very easy to manage...'

Angus smiled at the unrecognisable description of the wee rascals he had spanked soundly only that morning, but he did note that Ruby's sullen expression lightened at the mention of children.

'It'd be routine housework, Ruby,' he said. 'Dusting and cleaning, you know. My wife's a grand cook but she likes a little help in the kitchen now and again.'

Was that a fair description, he wondered, of washing dishes, cleaning pots, blacking ovens, peeling vegetables and all the other chores about which Lizzie constantly complained? Thinking back, Rowena had never complained.

'One of my workers married a lass from here – someone you might know,' he added. 'Rowena MacFarlane – well, Grey now.

195

Their cottage is just a stone's throw away from the farmhouse.'

To his surprise, it was as if someone had switched on a light behind her eyes. 'Ishbel?' she asked animatedly. 'How's the bairn?'

'Growing like a weed.'

'Right, I'll get my things!' she said decisively, and Angus was left wondering whether or not to tell his wife that her new maid only came so that she could renew her happy acquaintance with Rowena's baby...

On February 17th, 1900, wee Ishbel Grey happily celebrated her fourth birthday.

Miss Grey was a very important young lady, or so her daddy informed her. And her Grampa Tam – her favourite man in the world next to Daddy – her schoolteacher aunt, Sarah Grey, and Ruby Dunbar, all thought she was wonderful, too.

Her mother, whom Ishbel adored with a sometimes uncontrollable fierceness, tended to find occasional flaws in Miss Grey's perfection, but Jamie Campbell and Colin, his big brother, were always around to soothe away the pain of a smack with the assurance that 'all mothers are funny sometimes'.

They could not explain, though, why her Granny Grey from the Manse, a formidable lady, obviously liked her wee brother Simon better than her.

Ishbel loved wee Simon, too, so she didn't really mind Granny's preference for him. Anyway, Daddy had explained that grannies were like that.

He'd told her that Granny liked Daddy's wee boy best because she was Daddy's mother.

Unfortunately, Mama did not have a mother who would love a girl better, but at least Ishbel had Tam and Ruby to compensate.

'Wee Simon's a bobby dazzler right enough,' Ruby confided. 'But that's mostly because he's your wee brother, Ishbel.'

Perfect logic.

Miss Grey examined her petticoats and decided that she and they would be safer on Daddy's lap while they awaited the arrival of her birthday party guests.

Daddy was sitting in his big chair, but today he wasn't reading one of the books he and Mama read every single night after supper. Today, he was engrossed in the newspaper.

Maybe he would put it down if she asked him very, very nicely...

'Yes, as soon as Granny and Grampa and Aunt Sarah get here, I'll put it down, sweetheart. I promise,' Matt said, as he lifted her up on to the haven of his lap.

'But there's a war on, lambie, and Daddy has good friends who are soldiers. That's why I like to read the paper … to find out how they're getting on.'

And then he told her what a soldier was and all about the Boer War that had started last year, far, far away in Africa.

'After your party – or maybe tomorrow when I come in from the barn – we'll look up Africa in the atlas. You and Mama and me … all right?'

'Not Simon?'

'Och no – I don't think he'd be very interested,' Matt replied, dismissing the intellectual interests of his four-month-old son with just the hint of a smile.

Matt was understandably thrilled to be the father of a fine son, but, truth to tell, most of the time he forgot that this beautiful wee lass on his knees was not his own flesh and blood.

Ishbel was his 'sweetheart', the only person in the world who found him completely without fault. He loved her dearly.

He was trying to explain the position of the Boers as he saw it, when, through the window, he saw Ruby bustling down from the main house.

Ishbel saw her, too.

'Where's Grampa Tam?' she asked. 'He always hides when Ruby comes. But he likes her fine, Daddy. He's aye looking at her when he thinks she doesn't see him.'

Matt looked at his small daughter in amazement. He and Rowena had begun to notice the stirrings of courtship between Ruby and Tam.

But a small child being that perceptive took his breath away...

'You just watch what you're saying and mind your manners, Mistress Big Eyes,' he scolded, but Ishbel had jumped from his lap and scuttled across the room to greet Ruby's arrival.

'Ruby, Ruby, I'm four today!' she announced proudly. 'And Tam's helping in the scullery.'

'Happy birthday, ma wee darlin',' Ruby enthused, hugging Ishbel warmly. 'I widna' be surprised if there were presents for a birthday girl later on!'

'Tam's in the scullery, you say? Well, I'd better look in and gi'e him a wee hand. A hard-working man like Tam should be relaxing wi' his paper like your daddy.'

Ishbel stood stock still. Tam with his paper? Tam *never* read the paper. He sat night after night in the big chair with her or wee Simon on his lap and listened to Daddy read to Mama. Sometimes it was Mama who read.

She liked the books but Daddy often read from the newspaper. Mama and Tam would listen for a while, then Mama would say, 'Right, that's enough darlin'. Is the world not full of doom and gloom, Tam? Let's hear something from *Palgrave's Golden Treasury* instead.'

Ishbel loved trying to say *Palgrave's Golden Treasury*. It was such a long name for such a wee book. And she specially liked falling asleep with the horsey smell of Tam in her nostrils, while she listened to the soft voices of her parents.

Without looking, she could see the special smile on Daddy's face as he listened to Mama, and she could sense the warmth in Mama's eyes as she, in turn, listened to Daddy.

Oh, life was wonderful – and here at last was the pony and trap with Grampa and Granny Grey! And, joy of joys, Auntie Sarah was there, too!

She would be sure to have some sketching paper and some chalk with her. Ishbel would be able to draw Simon a really nice picture in the morning.

But before the morning, there was a cake with five candles to enjoy – one candle for each year of a very important person's life plus a fat pink one from Daddy 'to grow on.'

Miss Ishbel ran, not to her grandparents, but, in a flurry of yellow petticoats, to the scullery for Tam. *Now* the party could commence.

'I'm looking for a stallion for Bracken,' Tam

Laird announced later that same year to Matt. 'I'd like you to come with me to the Feein' Market in Forfar, lad. You can choose a good one.'

Shocked, Matt stood up from the fence against which he had been leaning with Tam. He looked into the field where Bracken, the late, lamented Fern's magnificent daughter, grazed placidly, while Ishbel, Colin, and James ran around her.

'But I wouldn't know what to look for in a stallion, Tam.'

'Then I've taught you nothin' in four years.'

'Oh, you know that's not true! I knew absolutely nothing four years ago and now... But a stallion's such a big investment–'

'Listen, lad, you have baith the book learning and the practical experience. Jist use your heid! Besides, I'll be there to hold your hand.

'We don't want to buy the beast, just rent its services. But for all that the Boss's money has to be well spent.'

Tam grinned at his protégé.

'Anyway do you think for a minute I'd let you make a mistake with my wee lass?'

Matt glanced across at Ishbel, his own wee lass.

'No, Tam.' He smiled. 'No man wants to make a mistake with anything so precious.

Right then, we'll both go to the Feein'
Market...'

On the day of the Market, however, Tam
woke with a raging fever.

'He's *definitely* not getting out of that bed!'
Rowena decreed. 'You'll have to go on your
own, Matt.'

Seeing the doubt in his eyes, she softened
her attitude... 'Listen, Tam trusts you, Matt.
You won't let him down.

'Anyway, I can't risk him getting pleurisy
again – for my own sake as well as his.'

'For your own sake?'

She smiled and tapped her stomach
gently. 'Well, it's too early to tell for sure...
Let's just say I'm too tired these days to
spend time nursing great, muckle men!'

With the promise in her eyes and her voice
warming his heart, Matt drove off alone to
Forfar in a light cart. The hint that they
were to be parents again had filled him with
confidence somehow.

He would look at the stallions, arrange a
date for Bracken to be serviced and hurry
back to his cottage, the home where
everything a man could possibly want was
waiting...

He remembered his first trip to the
Market when Marek MacFarlane had
stepped out from the side of the road and
levelled a gun at him.

It had taken him some sincere talking to convince the Romany that his cousin would be safe with Matt Grey.

Somehow Matt had known that this magnificent, menacing man would see through any glib promises or fancy talking. Only the truth would convince him.

'I fell in love with her the moment I saw her, man. Of course I'll look after her and her child,' Matt had assured him.

Marek had stared deeply into Matthew's eyes and had seen sincerity in them.

'Just see that you do, Gorgio, for I've loved Rowena all my life and that makes my claim stronger than yours.

'Remember this. If you harm so much as a hair on her head, I'll find you. No matter where you go, I'll track you down.

'I hear you like to gamble. Well, this time you're playing for the highest stakes of all – and the odds are in my favour. So be smart, Gorgio – and be lucky!'

With that, the Romany had kicked his horse round and taken his leave...

Well, thank goodness Marek and his threats were far away now. Today, there was nothing to delay Matt once his work at the Market was done.

He rode into the fairground and tethered his horse and cart.

He was leaning over a fence feeling at peace with the world when he heard his name being called.

'Good grief! Matt Grey as I live and breathe!'

Matt turned to see who'd greeted him, joy and hesitancy warring within him.

Before him, arms outstretched in welcome, stood the six feet three inches of Sergeant Donald Sinclair, the recruiting sergeant with the hardest head and strongest stomach in the British Army.

Well, what harm was there in having one drink with an old friend, maybe one hand of cards? Matt was surprised to realise that he missed the camaraderie of his old friends in the military.

For years now, he had been talking of nothing but babies and horses and weather. Intellectually, only Rowena was a match for him, since he saw so little of his father.

Their breach was healed but his mother could not soften her attitude to Ishbel – 'a tinker's bairn born out of wedlock' – and where Ishbel was unwelcome Matt would not go.

'Right, just one glass, Donald, and then I've work to do!'

'Ay, me, too,' the recruiting sergeant agreed quietly.

It was like old times. Laughter ensued and memories of comrades, some gone, some retired, several serving in this current, second Boer War in Africa – *'Thought we'd taken care of them at Majuba Hill back in '81, Matt. Apparently not, though.'*

One tankard of ale led to another, then another. And what harm could there be in just one more hand of cards...?

Eventually there was enough gold on the table in front of Matthew to send his children to university, to buy his beautiful wife a wardrobe of shop-made dresses and to buy, yes, to *buy* their own house, from which they could never be evicted.

The pot was enormous – and his hand was a good one.

There were only two players left in the game now, himself and the big recruiting sergeant.

Matt's head was spinning. He'd drunk too much and all of the considerable amount of cash he'd already won was now back on the table.

Seeing that Matt hadn't enough money left to bet with, his opponent offered him a deal.

'Think about it. One decent hand could set you up for life, Matt,' Donald Sinclair whispered temptingly.

'If you lose, though, you'll have to sign up here and now and you'll be off to fight the Boers! It's your choice, son.' The burly soldier chuckled drunkenly. 'Come on, lad – your Queen needs you.'

The voice echoed in his ear and sweat

beaded Matthew's forehead.

Your Queen needs you. Well, so do Rowena and wee Simon, his son, and Ishbel, the light of his life.

Off to fight the Boers. That was the gamble – but the cards he'd been dealt would be hard to beat… Should he bet or fold?

How often had he let the cards map out his life in the past? Too often perhaps. Yet Lady Luck had always smiled on him when he'd really needed her.

Should he gamble or walk away? Should he bet or fold?

Matt's hands trembled uncontrollably as, irrevocably, he reached the biggest decision of his young life…

Matt picked up his cards. He tried hard to still his trembling fingers. This was the best hand he'd ever had in a relatively-successful gambling career … but there was something unfathomable in Donald Sinclair's eyes.

The big sergeant wouldn't cheat, Matt was sure of that. No, he was safe, perfectly safe. Matt's hand was virtually unbeatable – he knew it, he felt it. So, gathering his wavering courage together, he turned over his cards for all to see…

'Well done, man!' someone yelled from the

crowd that had gathered round the table. They even began to stuff money into Matt's empty pockets.

'Ah, you showed him, lad! Your wife'll sleep comfortable tonight.'

'Except that those cards, Matt, my friend, *don't* beat mine.'

For a second, no more, Donald Sinclair looked slightly sorry, as he watched realisation dawn on his old friend and on the spectators.

'Four fours,' he said coldly. 'Sorry, Matt. Still, your loss is the British Army's gain, eh? I'll get you to sign up shortly.'

Four fours! Under Scots rules, this was the hand of hands. *This* was unbeatable.

Matt's entire body was trembling. How could he have been so stupid? How could he have risked his happiness with Rowena and the bairns?

Had he, deep down, rebelled against the backbreaking farm work, the dirt, the misery? Had he really *wanted* all along to join the army?

No – he loved his family more than anything...

He bit his lower lip in an attempt to keep his hand steady as he wrote *Matthew W Grey* on the official Army form. As he did so, he reflected sadly, that the last time he had signed anything like this it had been wee Simon's birth certificate.

Simon, Ishbel, Rowena. Better not to think about them...

'I think you owe me a wee dram, Donald. You can certainly afford it!' he said.

When it came, he tossed the amber liquid down as if it were sweet water from the burn.

Matt Grey drowned himself in *wee drams* over the next few weeks. He had written a cursory note to his Rowena explaining what had happened and after that had not been able to put pen to paper again.

She had written to him twice at the Army base and, amazingly, neither letter had been damning or accusing. Perhaps scorn or even hatred and anger would have been easier to handle...

Instead, Rowena had written of her understanding, her support, her promise to do the best for his children while he was away...

And now he lay with an aching head and mouth that seemed to be full of old horse blanket and his bed refused to stay still under him to let him sleep. Only in sleep was there sometimes the peace of oblivion.

At other times, though, he dreamed of Rowena as he had seen her that morning so long ago in his father's library. How lovely she had looked...

'Damn it all, what are they doing out there

that's making the barracks rock?' he asked and his answer was a dull laugh.

'Sober up, Private Grey! You're not in the blinkin' barracks! You're on a boat on your way to becoming a hero – if you don't drink yourself to death first, that is!'

Had the early summer ever looked lovelier? Rowena sighed as she hung out her washing and watched the long lines of garments begin to dance in the warm, south-western breeze.

The climbing roses at the door and against the stone wall were more vibrant, more abundant, more beautiful than they had ever been.

After four years of hard work and tender care, they were as glorious as she had dreamed they would be.

She brushed her hair away from her eyes and the sad thoughts from her mind. She would not wallow in misery. Such behaviour solved nothing.

Turning away from the washing lines, she caught sight of Tam Laird in the next field, whispering to Bracken. The fine, young Clydesdale mare occasionally threw up her head, as if she were listening to him and understanding every word.

Ruby Dunbar, unseen by Tam, was leaning against the gate watching man and horse – or possibly her eyes were lingering more on the man.

Feeling like an interloper, Rowena smiled and turned away. The lovelorn Ruby would have to work out the solution to her problem herself...

'Rowena, is the kettle on the fire?' Ruby hailed her, as she came bustling down the path from the Campbells' farmhouse, past the field where the horses grazed.

In her arms, was a heavy basket that would contain, no doubt, their month's ration of sugar and tea. Hidden underneath that, there would be something special for Ishbel and, maybe, for Tam.

'Is it ever *not* on?' Rowena asked as Ruby drew closer.

'Any word?' Ruby came straight to the point, as they headed into the cottage for a cup of tea.

'We're leaving, Ruby. I can't stay here. I think the Boss would let us, but our fine Christian mistress says she can't risk ruining Tam's reputation by having a woman whose husband is away, living with him.'

'Stupid wifie! Has she forgotten that you nursed Tam back to fitness for her? Does she no' feel she owes you anything?'

'No, she doesn't, Ruby. That apart, she's far too narrow minded! As if Tam Laird was in any danger from me, or me from him.'

Despite everything, Rowena managed a cheeky smile. 'Actually, I reckon he's in far more danger from you, if my eyes don't deceive me.'

Ruby coloured and hid her face in her teacup. 'Ach, he's a braw, gentle man, Rowena, but I suppose they a' change once they've walked you up that aisle!'

'No they don't! My Matt didn't change, Ruby, and neither would Tam.'

She looked straight at the other woman, making a serious point. 'It would be a pity if he was to move back into a bothy after four years of living in his own house.'

Ruby reached for the china teapot. 'Right enough... I'll think about that, see what I can do,' she said archly, her eyes twinkling.

At first, when Matt Grey had not returned to Springhill Farm, Angus Campbell had not been unduly concerned. He was used to the men going off to the Feein' Market and allowing themselves too much of a good time.

When the horse and cart he'd used were returned next day by a neighbouring farmer, his first impulse was to be furiously angry with Matt for being such a fool.

Then, when the enormity of what had happened had fully sunk in, his fear had been for Ishbel's future.

Lizzie had been furious. 'You shouldn't have let him go alone, Angus! It's all your fault. I suppose you'd better break the news to his tinker wife.

'But who's going to tell the Greys? They'll be distraught.'

'I suppose this Army business is legal,' Angus said, clutching at straws. 'There's no way we could say he was forced into joining up, is there? What was it they used to call it – "press ganged"?'

'No, by all accounts he was playing at cards perfectly willingly, Angus. Everyone was watching and apparently he was beaten fairly and squarely.

'He wasn't the only loser, though. You've lost a fine horseman, and with the harvest coming on, too.'

The harvest... Something else to worry about.

'Anyway, tell the gypsy woman she can have a few more days to make her arrangements, Angus.'

Angus stood stock still, as if turned to stone. He was devastated. He could not even turn to look at his wife.

'Arrangements?' he repeated, still with his back to her.

'Well, she can't stay there – housekeeper to an unmarried man. It's not on! People would talk and there's been more than enough of that lately.'

Angus turned at last. 'Lizzie, do you hear what you're saying? Rowena Grey's man has gone to the war and you'd have me throw her and her bairns out in the road.'

'They're the minister's problem now, Angus, not ours.' Her expression was determined. 'I'm thinking of the Greys, too.

'They were unhappy about the marriage and about their boy becoming a farm labourer, but the hoo-ha has all died down now.

'Matthew's earned a place here and he's good at his job. In time, he could be almost as good with horses as Tam.

'But he's just showed us all that the old Matt was there all the time, sleeping under the respectable coat.

'The whole parish will be talking and the minister and his wife won't want to listen to folk saying their son's wife's no better than she should be. They'll be hoping all the talk has died down for good.'

'Like I say, that gypsy would be better wi' her own kind – far away from us and the Greys.'

She was right, of course, horribly right. There had been a great deal of talk about the marriage of the kitchen maid and the minister's only son.

By sheer hard work, though, the young couple had made themselves respected – and now Matt had shattered all that.

But Angus could not throw out Ishbel. That was unthinkable. She was *his* child – his only daughter...

'I'll away down and have a word with her, Lizzie, but we'll have to think of something.

'Maybe Rowena could stay on in the cottage with the bairns and Tam could go back to the bothy. He's been living like a king for four years now, you know.'

Angus stomped off and Lizzie watched him go. She smiled faintly to herself.

She had wanted rid of the MacFarlane woman for years and now, at last, everything was working out properly.

She would let Ruby look after Tam. That way he could stay on in his cottage. Why should Tam have to give up his home?

Ruby Dunbar was a good worker and could easily manage the cottage as well as the main house. Goodness, with both boys at school all day, there was hardly enough work to keep her occupied!

Walter Grey simply told his wife that Matt had joined the army. He tried not to tell her the full truth: that Matt had started drinking and gambling again.

Instead, he reminded her of all the military friends their son had had throughout the years.

'It's all this Boer War publicity, Chrissie. Young men see only the glory in war. They don't see the pain and fear.

'In a rash moment, he obviously listened to all the fine words of a recruiting sergeant at the Market.

'You'll see, when he writes to poor Rowena ... he'll admit that he acted stupidly and has made a terrible mistake.'

Chrissie looked at him out of tear-drenched eyes, in which a tiny flame of hope had been rekindled.

'Then he'll come home, Walter? You'll explain to the powers-that-be that he didn't mean to join the army, that he's a married man with a baby, won't you?

'You'll explain and make it all right, Walter. You're a minister – a man of good standing...'

He shook his head sadly. 'I'm afraid there's nothing I can do. After all, he wasn't coerced, my dear. He signed of his own free will.'

He dared not add that it was all down to a lost wager.

Chrissie began to wail again and rocked herself back and forth in her misery.

'It was her, that MacFarlane woman, wasn't it? She made Matthew miserable, so he's joined the army to be free of her.'

Walter Grey let her spill out all her vitriol. When she was calm, she would admit that Matt had genuinely loved his wife and the children.

But for now she needed to be allowed to blame someone, anyone, besides her son...

He went into the kitchen and asked old

Elsie the housekeeper to make them some hot tea. She was also deeply upset and he tried to comfort her, too.

'That cottage they live in, it's tied, isn't it, Reverend? With Matthew gone, the farmer will want the place back for a working family, won't he?'

Walter had not thought of all the ramifications of Matt's actions, but Elsie was right. The cottage was tied to the job and now the workman was away.

Rowena could not have done her husband's job, even if there hadn't been two small children underfoot...

A little later, Walter's hands shook slightly, as he poured his wife a restoring cup of tea.

'There, is that better, my dear? Now, I'd like you to rest for the afternoon – try to get some sleep – while I go up and visit our daughter-in-law.

'We must find out what her plans are.'

At that, Chrissie Grey sat bolt upright. 'Plans? What plans could she have but to look after the children until Matthew comes home? We don't even know how long he's signed up for.

'Is he only a soldier for the duration of this war? Well, it's over now, isn't it? Didn't we read about the relief of some important place? Yes, Mafeking, that was it!'

Chrissie felt a slight easing of her tension. Of course, of course, it was over out there.

It was all over and Matt would come home and, oh, how she would scold him, silly boy!

Then she remembered that he had signed a paper and the horror returned. 'But, Walter, he might have signed up for ten years – or for all his working life! My poor boy.

'Anyway, that wife of his can have no plans but to wait, like better women before her.'

Obviously, this was not the time to speak about tied cottages. He would just have to have a quiet word with Angus Campbell, who would, no doubt, be as anxious as he was not to lose Rowena.

At his first port of call, Rowena invited Walter Grey in to the spotlessly-clean front room as welcomingly as she had ever done.

Apart from shadows of tiredness under the fine, dark eyes and a paler complexion than usual, she looked just as beautiful as ever.

Ishbel, his pretty granddaughter, ran to meet him and he picked her up in his arms and sat with her on his lap while he drank the tea that Rowena had insisted on pouring.

'Little pitchers, Ishbel,' Rowena said with a smile.

'That means you can't talk, Grampa,' Miss Grey explained. 'Mama always says "little pitchers" when Daddy's not supposed to talk.'

Her expression grew more serious. 'He never came home from the Market, you know. The bothy lads think he's in jail, drunk. And they should–'

'That's quite enough, Madame, if you don't want your tongue scrubbed with carbolic soap!'

For the first time, Rowena sighed wearily. 'I'm afraid we've spoiled her, Mr Grey.'

'Matt probably has, my dear. But she's pretty hard to resist, isn't she?'

'Listen, perhaps we'd be better to talk alone...' He gestured towards the other door.

'Right – Ishbel, go and watch wee Simon until he wakes. No, don't argue, please. Just do it!'

As soon as the little girl was out of earshot, Walter moved his chair closer to his daughter-in-law's. Over the past four years, he had come to respect and admire her, even to like her.

She made Matt happy and she kept a beautiful home, in which she seemed, magically, to make every penny do the job of a shilling.

'Rowena, I can't say how sorry I am about all this.'

She inclined her head in an almost regal fashion.

'Has – has Mr Campbell spoken to you?' he asked.

'Just to tell me Matt's gone off to be a soldier.'

Walter was quiet, deep in thought. Would he be better to say nothing of his worries?

'Listen, I know fine well what's bothering you, Reverend. This is Tam Laird's cottage and my man has gone.

'I doubt if the good folk around here would be happy about an old bachelor and a married woman living together – no matter how innocent or convenient it was.

'No, we'll have to leave, me and my children. That's all there is to it.'

'Have you anywhere to go?'

Rowena laughed, throwing her head back and showing him her fine white teeth.

'No doubt my man will send me his wages. Isn't that the army way? I'm sure we won't starve.'

'Listen, I'll have a word with Mr Campbell...'

'What – and wreck another marriage? I don't think so. His good lady isn't exactly my greatest admirer.

'No, there's no way that we can stay here without Matt's protection.'

Matt's protection. She had not thought of that aspect of marriage before, but, of course, Matt's name, his presence, even his job, protected her.

'I just hope Ruby will move in to take care of Tam,' Rowena added philosophically.

Walter was shocked for a moment, then he realised what she meant.

'Is that how the wind's blowing? Well, it would probably be good for both of them.

'Ruby has blossomed here since her workhouse days, and Tam's fitter than ever he was, thanks to your care, Rowena.'

'Ay, and the same Tam's well aware – as naebody else seems tae be – of whit he owes this fine lassie!'

An angry Tam Laird was suddenly in the room. Neither of them had heard him approach.

'Rowena, lass,' he said firmly, 'this is your home and they'll drive you out of it o'er my dead body! It's only evil minds as would think there's anything wrang wi' you stayin' here till your man comes hame.'

'Right, sit down, Tam, please – and listen,' the minister urged soothingly. 'Your feelings do you credit, man, but think about it. Maybe those narrow-minded folk you're decrying are actually thinking of Rowena's reputation.

'She's the mother of young children and she shouldn't be "living in" as the house-keeper to an unmarried man, should she?'

Tam carefully wiped his hands on his trousers before taking the cup of tea that Rowena handed him. He looked at the minister shrewdly.

'Ach, I suppose you're right, Meenister. But if the lassie cannae bide wi' me, she'll just hae to go to her man's family, won't she?

'There's the answer, Rowena lass, although it'll break my heart to part with you and the bairns. No, you go and live in that nice, big Manse. There'll be plenty of room there.

'That'll pit a stop tae any talk in the valley!' He smiled as he looked at Matt's father. 'Cat got your tongue, Reverend?'

'Tam,' Rowena rescued her father-in-law, who was squirming with embarrassment, 'that wouldn't be fitting. A lass like me can't bide in a Manse!'

Walter Grey stood up. He was a little pale but otherwise in control. 'Actually, in fact Tam's absolutely right, my dear. Where else should you go but to your husband's family? Simon ... the children are *our* grandchildren, and you are *our* son's wife.

'You'll excuse me now, please, while I go and have a word with Mr Campbell.

'Then I'll head home to ask Mrs Grey to prepare some rooms to welcome you.'

Rowena tried to protest. She saw so many problems looming ahead. Deep down, she wished that all these well-meaning people would just give her some peace and quiet – and time alone to think.

'Let the Reverend go, Rowena,' Tam said,

'and I'll hae one of thae scones. I'll miss your baking, lass.'

But Rowena was watching Matt's father walking, head bowed, up to the farmhouse.

He wants me at the Manse as much as I want to go there, she thought – but, in fact, that wasn't true.

Walter's first reaction to Tam's words was that, of course, in all conscience, Rowena and the children *must* move in with them.

There was more than enough room; it was the truly Christian thing to do...

But then, immediately following that thought, had come the bitter memory of Chrissie blaming Rowena for Matt's enlistment.

How could these two women possibly live together for years?

He would talk to Angus, see if there was another cottage that could be given to Rowena.

If that failed, he would just have to talk to Chrissie and try to convince her that Rowena sharing their home was a practical and Christian idea.

For a start, if Matthew's wife was welcomed into his parents' home, they would almost certainly know where their son was.

Walter knew that his son loved Rowena and the children. He would write to her very regularly and, hopefully, Rowena would share his news with them.

The second plus point was Simon. He was Chrissie's adored little grandson. If he was living in her home, she might be allowed some say in his upbringing.

Even if she was not, she would certainly be there for every precious moment of his growing. She would hear his first word, see his first, faltering steps...

That picture was so entrancing that Walter found his steps speeding up.

The Manse was so big and sprawling that the children and their mother could have their own quarters well away from the Greys. That way, all their noise and carrying-on wouldn't be a problem.

In other words, if they put them far enough away, Granny and Grampa would still get their much-needed sleep!

The only problem, and it was surely very slight, was Ishbel. It had to be admitted that Chrissie did not have the same feeling for the wee lass as she had for her half-brother.

Ach, but that'll change, Walter told himself, a bit desperately. *Chrissie'll grow to love the wee lass when she's in the house with her all the time. We'll be one big happy family...*

The African sun stared at them out of a cloudless sky, just as it had done the day before and the day before that. The news of

Mafeking had not yet reached this distant outpost.

It was evening and the British troops prepared for another night under siege.

'You know, Scottie, when I get back home, I don't think as I'll ever complain about the soft mists of rain again.'

Matt Grey looked at the young Welsh soldier who was sharing this watch with him and wiped the sweat from his face with a dirty cloth before replying.

'Easy seen you're a taffy, Bryn! There's no such thing as *soft mists* where I come from in Scotland. The rain comes bucketing down in sheets and sometimes bounces back up just as high!'

'Is it strong enough to wash the sand out from under this blasted shirt?' Bryn asked. 'I think I can bear anything but the way it creeps into every nook and cranny! I'm red raw, man.

'My face and hands are raw from the heat of the sun and my back is chaffed by the damn sand!'

'Join the army! See yourself in a fine red jacket! See the wonders of the world!' Matt quoted bitterly. 'Well, you wanted this, lad.

'Me, I'm here by mistake. Besides, I never saw soldiering as holding women and children in a prison camp to make their menfolk do what we want them to do. That can't be right.'

The British Army had, indeed, concentrated the families of Boers in camps and Matt and what was left of the small garrisons were in charge of one of the prison camps.

Soldiers in confinement, prisoners of war, was one thing. Imprisoning old women, young mothers and children – dash it all, that wasn't soldiering!

'So you don't want to be a soldier, Scottie?' Bryn Cordell's voice broke into his thoughts.

'Well, if I had a lovely wife and a couple of children by my fireside like you have, I'd never have left them. You're a fool, Matt.'

Matt did not argue. He *was* a fool and more than a fool because he hadn't even written to Rowena since he'd been posted here. He sent his pay packet every week so she knew he was alive, but what could he possibly say to her?

His fingers smoothed the pages of her letters inside the breast pocket of his tunic. Her words were so loving and trusting and forgiving...

Wee Simon was walking. They were very happy at the Manse. He wondered about how much credence to give to that claim. *Ishbel was going to school in the autumn.*

There was even a letter from Ishbel tucked in beside her mother's letters. What a clever lass! It had been written on what looked like the page of an old sermon.

No doubt Matt's father had finished with it.

'Here comes the water, Bryn lad,' he said and they stood together watching, relieved, as young Private Singer came round with the night's drinking ration.

The sky was darker now, the sun less fierce.

'You're allowed one quarter of a cup each. I'd make it last, boys. They say there'll be no supplies through for a few days yet.'

No, of course there would be no supplies through.

The Boer Army was teasing them. Sometimes the enemy soldiers even allowed themselves to be seen, standing like a forest of trees on a distant hill.

They were making the point that, for once, they easily outnumbered the British forces and could overpower them whenever they wanted.

Then, as the exhausted Brits watched, they would melt away without a sound so that our lads were left wondering whether or not they'd imagined everything...

So far, the Boer snipers had picked them off ruthlessly, one at a time. The British infantryman was trained to face large-scale attack; he could not cope with death that struck without warning, from the roof of a church, from the branches of a tree...

Matt sighed. There was no way out. They were trapped, pinned down. He knew it. His comrades knew it. The Boers knew it.

Only Sergeant Walker, the senior man left in command, seemed *not* to know it.

'They'll get through to us, boys,' he said over and over again, until maybe he believed it. A few of the very young lads believed it, too, because they wanted to, because they had to.

'The Army knows that we're here. They'll send reinforcements soon.'

'In time to sweep up the bits,' Bryn muttered...

At last, night fell and they had to wrap themselves up against the unbelievable cold that always followed the blistering heat of the day.

'Can't think why anyone would want to live in a hell-hole like this, Scottie lad,' Bryn moaned. 'It burns the skin off you all day and freezes the blood in your veins all night!

'Give me the Brecons any day, bach.'

Matt remembered his trek over countless miles of rolling plains under vast, blue skies and smiled. He could easily understand the pull of Africa. In another life, he would have enjoyed exploring it, like David Livingstone.

'We're not fightin' for the land, Bryn,' he replied. 'All this is about money. Isn't it always the—'

'Right,' a strident voice suddenly interrupted, 'when you two lads have finished your philosophising, I'd like a moment of your valuable time!'

Sergeant Walker had come into the guard-room, where Bryn and Matt were sharing their small ration of food.

'Aw, Sarge, and we'd just decided to nip down to the pub for a swift half!' Matt quipped.

'I'm glad you can still laugh, Private Grey,' the burly sergeant replied. ''Cause I'm damned if I can. I reckon we're in deep trouble.

'They're going to overrun us soon. I can feel it. If reinforcements don't get here in the next few hours, we're done for.'

'Tell us something we don't know.'

'Well, how about this? I'm making Grey here a lance-corporal – a field promotion you might call it.'

Matt said nothing. A promotion? Why? Maybe so that Rowena would get a few more shillings if he died in action – that is, if anyone ever heard he had been promoted...

'Why, Sarge?' he asked eventually.

'Because we can't afford to wait any longer, lad. If nothing happens soon, I'm going over the wall to look for the reinforcements.

'I figure if I ride hell for leather, I might just outdistance the Boers. Anyway, your promotion would leave you as the senior rank here, Grey. You'd be in charge.'

'But, Sarge, I haven't even been in for a year yet! I'm not a proper soldier. I'm a farm worker pretending to be a soldier.

'Besides, I hate to remind you, but I'm more at home on a horse than either you or young Bryn here.'

'Ay, that's true, but you're also a born leader, Matt, and you've got education. I know the Captain, God rest his soul, was going to give you a stripe. He told me just a few hours before he was killed.'

The Captain. Matt's heart swelled with pride. The Captain had thought well of him.

Oh, how proud Rowena would be – and his parents. He could practically hear his mother boasting, *'My boy's been promoted...'*

If he did not get killed first.

'Thanks, Sarge. It means a lot to me. Right, I'm going to write to my wife now.

'After that, maybe we could have a hand or two of cards, eh? Or a throw of the dice? You know, something to distract us while we're waiting.'

He sat down at the table and took out the writing paper which had been used so little over the recent months. When he did start to put pen to paper, the words positively spilled out.

My darling wife,
How can I ask you to forgive me for not

writing for so long? The truth is, I was too ashamed. I acted like an idiot – and, unfortunately, I've paid the price. I'm so sorry.

I miss you all so much. Words can't express how much I long to be with you, my love; how much I long to see our babies.

Are we to be blessed with another soon? I do hope so...

Forgive me, Rowena, and remember this – no matter what happens, you are all to me that any man could ask.

The four wonderful years of our marriage pass before my eyes night and day in this strange, foreign land. There's no pain in the memories, only warmth and laughter and love.

Was I ever cold or hungry or tired? No, because at the end of each day no matter what I'd had to cope with on the farm, there was always you ... my warmth, my sustenance, my life. My Rowena.

Kiss my lovely daughter for me and tell her I want her to grow up to be exactly like her mother.

And my son, my little boy... Make a better man of him than his father ever was.

Things are pretty bad here, I'm afraid. Thoughts of all of you and of home are a real comfort. No matter what happens, I hope you'll think of me kindly and be able to forgive my many weaknesses.

Oh, by the way, I'm to be promoted! Lance-corporal Grey. Sounds all right, doesn't it? Hope you're proud of me. I am fiercely proud of you.

I hope you're settling in at the Manse and coping with everything – especially my parents. They mean well. Give them my love, too.

Better go, my darling. Duty calls and all that. Be strong and be happy. Try to think fondly of me.

I love you. I always will.

Your devoted husband,

Matthew Grey.

He sealed the letter and set it on the table for someone, preferably himself, to post.

And then he took the dice from a pocket in his kit bag…

'Come on, Sarge,' he said, 'have you ever played for *really* high stakes? The future of the world can depend on the roll of the dice, you know.'

'What are you on about, lad?' the older, seasoned campaigner asked. 'Money hardly matters to us now.'

'I'm not talking about money. I'm talking about which one of us goes over the wall, Sarge…

'No, hold on!' Matt insisted as Sergeant Walker began to protest. 'We could argue about this until we're blue in the face…

'You reckon I'd be fine left in command. I *know* the lads would rather face the Boer with you leading them. That's a fact.

'The other indisputable fact is that I'm a better horseman than you. I've been taught

by Tam Laird – the best in the business…
I'd have a much better chance than you of
reaching the relief force.'

'Maybe so, Matt, but the bitter truth is
that even the Queen's top jockey mounted
up on the blinkin' Derby winner wouldn't
have a cat in hell's chance of getting past
them Boer snipers.

'Whoever goes out there is riding into
almost-certain death.'

The two men, comrades in arms, friends
in adversity, exchanged knowing glances.
Each saw respect in the other's eyes.

'So are you ready to play, Sarge?' Matt
asked. 'Highest score rides out.'

Rather wanly, the older man smiled.
'Right, lad – you throw first.'

A jackal cried eerily in the African night,
as Matthew Grey shook the dice in the palm
of his right hand…

The roses were gone. Even the brambles
had been harvested in rich, ripe clusters
from the hedgerows.

Rowan berries hung on frail stalks from
the branches of the Mountain Ash and fat
hips swelled where, just a few weeks ago,
wild roses had held their delicate faces to
the late summer sun.

Autumn was here. The harvest was in the barns, but Rowena had not danced in the bothy this year.

Since her husband had left Springhill Farm to be a soldier, she was no longer an orraman's wife ... she was now Mrs Matthew Grey, who resided at the Manse with her in-laws.

It would have been unfitting for the daughter-in-law of the Manse to whirl the hours away at a harvest dance.

Besides, and Rowena smiled and touched her stomach lightly, she was in a delicate condition. There was definitely another baby on the way.

Her letter to Matt confirming this good news would certainly force a reply from him. Rowena knew her husband. She was sensitive to his shame and knew that it would take time for him to work it out of his system.

She was content – no, not content, resigned – to writing to him, to reassure him of her faith in him, her love for him. For, truly, her love had grown so strongly and steadily as the roses in her recent garden.

She had almost forgotten that moment of madness all those years ago when she had allowed herself to pretend, for just one magic evening, that she and Angus Campbell were both free.

She had forgiven the farmer for abandoning her and she had accepted that his love for their daughter was genuine.

Ishbel belonged here at Springhill as obviously as she did not.

'Good morning, Mistress Grey,' someone said.

'Good morning,' Rowena replied pleasantly. She loved this interaction with the people of the valley.

She was *Mistress* Matthew Grey, daughter-in-law of the Manse and one day soon, please God, her Matt would return, brown as a nut, from the African sun.

She was going to buy some ribbons to trim the baby dresses that both she and her sister-in-law Sarah were making for the new arrival. It was a joy to have Sarah Grey as a friend, even though Rowena could not understand it sometimes.

Sarah loved Matt. Therefore anything her brother loved would be tolerated by Sarah. But there was more to it than that. The educated daughter of the Manse really liked her sister-in-law.

'You're a fascinating person, my dear. A gypsy who reads Chaucer, and actually understands him! You Irish are an amazing race, aren't you?'

Rowena had laughed at that. In truth, she was more *Romany* than Irish, but dear Sarah didn't seem to want to acknowledge that part of her ancestry.

She was still chuckling at the memory

when she reached the post office, where she had promised to buy a stamp for Matt's father.

'A stamp for a letter to Africa, please, Mrs Ramsay,' she said, putting her money down on the mahogany counter.

The postmaster's wife looked at her quizzically and her bright blue eyes clouded over. 'What to South Africa, Mistress Grey? Oh, lassie,' she said sadly, 'you've surely no' looked at the windae.'

Rowena felt the dart pierce her heart. The windae! Officers wives, naturally being of superior stock, received telegrams at home. Enlisted men's wives had to read their man's fate in the post office window.

Picking up her pennies, she walked outside. The name Grey was approximately a third of the way down the short list.

Lance-Corporal Matthew Walter Grey.

Rowena's stunned mind fixed on the inessentials. Matt was a corporal. He must have been promoted. How proud his parents would be...

The autumn air outside the village post office was just as fragrant, just as redolent of autumn's glories, as it had been an hour before.

But Matt – her dear, sweet Matt – was dead.

Real life is never all misery; neither is it all

joy. It is a glorious mixture. Matt Grey was dead. The handsome young soldier had died a hero.

They had learned that he had fallen to a sniper's bullet while riding out to try to save his comrades. His heavily-pregnant wife had been told that she would receive a medal to honour his last act of supreme bravery.

The award, special though it was, was scant compensation for the loss of a beautiful, loving husband and father...

Elsewhere, though, life was taking a happier turn. At an age when most men were thinking of taking retirement, Matthew Grey's old friend and mentor, Tam Laird, was taking a wife.

Tam sat in the bathtub on his last morning of bachelorhood, and thought about his past and his future.

Never before had he regarded the love of a woman as being more important than his beloved Clydesdales. In his heart, he had loved Rowena Grey. In fact, he still did and always would – but he had never wanted to wed her. She was too ... disturbing.

And now Ruby had come in to his life. Sitting in his scalding hot bath, Tam thought of Ruby as he scrubbed his back, and he laughed.

Ruby. Ruby. She was as different to Rowena as wee Bracken, his favourite filly, was to a cow!

Through the steam, he could see the hills covered in their autumn colours.

We're in the autumn of our days, my Ruby and me, he thought. All our fires are burned out, but the harvest of all our years is safely gathered inside us.

She'll care for me and I – what was it the meenester said at weddings? – I will cleave tae her and care for her till death (that's probably no' that far away, though I've cheated it a time or two) parts us.

Ruby's a grand woman. No' a patch on Rowena for looks, but then I'm no oil painting mysel' and she seems content.

I'll never let her down, mind, but it's a pity that we've left it too late – that there'll never be a bairn in our house…

Tam dressed in his brand-new suit, which, when he returned from the wedding, he would put straight into the kist for his winding sheet, and went out to meet his employer.

Angus Campbell, thinner and quieter than he had ever been, was waiting to drive his first horseman to the wee church, where the Reverend Walter Grey would conduct the wedding service.

They spoke little on the short journey.

Suddenly there was the church and, at the door, all Tam's friends, looking uncharacteristically and uncomfortably smart in their best suits.

The odd smile greeted their arrival, but, surprisingly, the solemnity of the setting seemed to have got to the farm workers and there was none of the ribald banter they'd half expected.

'Don't worry – we'll cheer 'em up later, Tam,' Angus quipped. 'There's enough whisky back at the farm to float a wreck on the Tay!'

Tam turned and looked at his employer, his best man, whom he knew so well. He smiled warmly. 'I'm marrying Ruby Dunbar, Maister, and I love her richt weel. She means the world to me.

'But I'll never forget the way that Rowena MacFarlane welcomed me into her house and her family and nursed me back to health. So I just want you to know that I'll watch out for her and her bairns as long as I can draw breath.'

Angus smiled. He said nothing, but his heart spoke and Tam heard it.

Me, too, it said. *For all the days of my life.*

'Rowena, if you can't keep that child quiet, please take him to your own rooms.'

Him, not *her* for once. So even Simon was beginning to annoy his grandparents...

Oh, they were not unfeeling folk. They were not unkind. They were not un-Christian.

Truth to tell, they were just old.

Small children make a great deal of noise. Wee Simon crying in the night *was* disturbing.

It was amazing how the sound of even so small a child could cut through the thick walls of such an old house.

And Ishbel? She was precocious. She could write; she could draw.

But how many times could even the most devoted of grandpas summon patience when she scribbled her latest masterpiece on a page of a sermon over which the minister had laboured far into the night?

And she's not even related to us! Complained an angry, unwanted voice within him.

The Reverend Walter Grey looked at himself in the shaving mirror and did not like what he saw. He had aged. That was perfectly understandable, though.

After all, his only son was a victim of this new – what was it they called it in *The Courier?* – Guerilla Warfare.

Yes, that was it! It was when fighting men did not stand face to face any longer, but sneaked up on one another instead, and killed without warning from hidden places...

Walter had wanted, all his life, to do the right thing by his God and by his monarch. But this latest duty – looking after his beloved boy's family – was so hard...

Chrissie had taken to her bed again when

Rowena, distraught, had brought back the shocking news of Matthew's death.

For all her weaknesses, Chrissie had loved Matthew as dearly as any mother could love a son. He had settled down so well latterly that it had been hard not to admire him, almost impossible to recall his unchristian past.

Had Matthew been an officer, as his birth and education merited, they would have received a telegram. The post office window was yet one more indignity.

He had died a hero, though, which filled his father's heart with pride – and restored his faith in the boy who, despite their vast differences, Walter had always adored.

But not even heroes, it seemed, were worth the price of a telegram...

Rowena had kept the news of their second – no, no, there was Ishbel, whom Matt had loved as if she were his own – their *third* grandchild from them as long as possible.

Bowed down by grief and pregnancy and, no doubt by fear for her future, the young widow had looked after Chrissie as patiently and lovingly as Sarah would have done had she not been out all day teaching.

And still Chrissie refused to get well. And that was the heart of the matter. She was *refusing* to get well.

Dear God, was she enjoying being a martyred mother? Not his Chrissie. Surely not? And what would happen when Rowena's time was due?

Sighing, Walter returned to his sermon. He still had other souls to comfort.

How often had he counselled others to keep their faith in the goodness of God, no matter how cruel the world seemed in its darkest hours?

Now he was having to practise what he preached. He prayed for the strength to do just that...

'Lord, forgive my doubts and weakness. I pray that You mould me, use me and give me the courage to carry on. I am in Your hands.'

'I'm leaving, Angus.' Rowena stood before the farmer, looking just as enchanting, as desirable as she had on that fateful, long-ago summer evening. Yet she had changed.

There was no love in her eyes for him now, no respect even. He had lost that years ago, he knew, when he had refused to acknowledge his child and had condemned her to the Woman's Refuge.

There was no way of measuring what that act of betrayal had cost her.

Now he had no weapons to use against her, no strength to call on. She was leaving and that meant he would lose the daughter, the tow-headed little charmer who smiled down at him warmly as she sat, like a queen, on the back of one of Tam's horses...

241

'Rowena, you can't mean it,' Angus finally managed to say. 'Where on earth would you go?'

'I mean it all right! I can't stay here like this,' she said. 'Matthew's parents don't mean to be unkind but the children are so small and so...' She shrugged. 'Ach, they're just children – normal, noisy bairns.

'And soon there will be another and that'll be too much for the Greys.

'No, my mind's made up. I'll return to my own people.'

He hardly dared speak. 'Where?'

'This year they're in Ireland. It's a fine country. My children will grow strong there.'

'Ishbel?' he breathed.

Her face was sad. 'She is my heart, Angus.'

He had to do something, say something. There had to be a way out. My God, he was exactly where he had been nearly five years before.

This time, though, he could not expect her to make any concessions.

'She's my daughter, too, Rowena.'

She was close to the birth of her late husband's baby, but she still drew herself up proudly.

'Ay, she is. So I take it that you'll acknowledge her, Angus, give her her rightful place?'

How could he? It was unfair to ask. Lizzie would never forgive him and there were the boys to think about and the farm, his farm – the farm he had laboured to make profitable.

She looked into his eyes and saw all his weakness. Smiling, she turned, and, without another word, walked away.

The thought of losing his only daughter tortured Angus's soul. He couldn't bear to be without Ishbel, no matter what.

At the last minute, he ran after her.

'Listen, we can't leave it like that. I'll tell you what – I'll draw up a legal document, Rowena.

'Ishbel is my daughter after all and I want her to have exactly the same rights as her half-brothers.

'So, on Christmas Eve, at the watchnight service, I'll give you a paper outlining my daughter's future. All right?'

Did she believe him? Had she taken in the generosity of his offer? Angus simply didn't know.

All he could do now was watch her walk away slowly into the darkness of a cold, December evening...

As always, it was the children who waited anxiously for the Christmas festivities to start. The choir had been rehearsing carols for weeks, all the old favourites, *Hark The Herald Angels Sing,* and *Silent Night,* among them.

Walter Grey sat in the back of his chilly little church and wondered at the glorious sounds being produced by rough farm lads and flighty shop girls.

There was real talent there, but it would never be heard by anyone except other farmers. And, sadly, that was the way it had always been.

In this new century, Walter began to wonder at the rightness of things.

Ishbel sat beside him in her new green coat, then climbed on to his lap. He held the small, warm body close for a moment. He could well understand how Matt had loved this child with her open, smiling ways – even though he had not been her natural father.

'We'd better be getting home, Ishbel,' he whispered into the shell-like little ear. 'Your Aunt Sarah will probably need your help with Simon.'

'No, Simon'll prob'ly need my help with Aunt Sarah!' she whispered back and the blue eyes were dancing with mischief.

He held her hand as she skipped beside him in the frosty moonlight.

Every light in the Manse was on and Walter knew exactly what that meant.

Rowena's baby had obviously decided to come early and old Elsie, the housekeeper, and Ruby Laird from the farm – both steeped in the old superstitions – would have 'no shadows in the infant's way.'

It was an easy birth, as Simon's had been, and just before he left for the watchnight service, Walter blessed his brand-new granddaughter and her exhausted mother.

'Take Ishbel to the kirk with you, Reverend,' Rowena pleaded. 'It's important...'

And so Angus Campbell with his wife, Lizzie, and their two sons beside him and his servants behind him, saw wee Ishbel Grey nod with weariness against her maiden Aunt Sarah's black coat.

At the end of that most joyous of services, Tam Laird strode forward to relieve the schoolma'am of her precious bundle.

'We'll walk back wi' you, Miss Sarah,' he said shyly. 'I'll carry the bairn. She's quite an armful is our Ishbel.'

In her sleep, Ishbel heard Tam's beloved voice and nestled against him happily. To the wee lass, Tam and Ruby were goodness personified.

Angus Campbell stood up. He had made a promise to Rowena and he had kept his word, but she was not here. He wasn't sure what to do now.

Perhaps she had changed her mind. Maybe she wasn't going to leave after all.

Then he remembered the determination in her face and her voice... No, she would not be deflected from her purpose.

He left his wife and his two sons and went

over to speak to Sarah Grey.

She looked surprised to see him approach.

'Em, hello, Miss Grey,' he began awkwardly. 'Merry Christmas to you.'

'And to you,' she replied.

'The thing is, I was wondering … is Rowena, em, Mrs Grey not here tonight?'

'No, my sister-in-law is confined,' she said. 'She has just been blessed with another daughter.'

Muttering his congratulations, Angus then pulled a parchment from the breast pocket of his Sunday suit and gave it to her.

'I wonder if you'd be so kind as to give her this, please?'

But before Sarah could reply, he had turned back to his waiting family.

Less than three short weeks later, Rowena Grey disembarked from the boat that had carried her over to Ireland.

She tried not to dwell on what she'd done, concentrating only on feeding her new baby and pacifying wee Simon as best she could.

It had been the right decision – but that hadn't made it any easier. In fact, it was the hardest thing she had ever done in her life…

If she thought about Ishbel waking up in Tam and Ruby's cottage and realising that her mother and her wee brother and sister were gone, she would dissolve in tears and she didn't have time for tears.

In her pocket was the letter from Angus that Sarah had given her.

I, Angus Campbell, it read, *do solemnly swear before God that I am the father of Ishbel Grey, daughter of Rowena MacFarlane Grey.*

As my daughter, Ishbel is entitled to a daughter's share of my farm, Springhill, and so I have informed my solicitor.

Signed on this 24th day of December, nineteen hundred and one.

Oh, Ishbel, my darling, forgive me, she prayed silently. My heart is broken, but I can't take you away from what is rightfully yours. Ruby and Tam will raise you as if you were their own. You'll be their joy; you'll make their happiness complete.

And don't worry about your brother and sister. I'll love them and Marek will protect us all. One day, hopefully, their grandparents will see them again.

She thought about that, about the difficulties of generations trying to live together. About old people, used to peace and quiet, suddenly being faced with boisterous youngsters who brought not only love in to their lives but also chaos.

Perhaps if she had not been who she was... Perhaps when Matt's mother had got over his death, if she ever did, maybe then they would have been able to lead some kind of life where the children would have been more welcome...

Her heart ached from the pain of it all. She still hadn't come to terms with the loss of Matthew, the man she had loved above all. Her dear, handsome husband.

But she had such memories of him still – sweet, unforgettable memories – of his smile, of his determination, of his loving and of his last, beautiful letter to her...

She looked through the mist. Marek would come soon.

Was that him appearing through the rain? She eased the baby on her hip. Soon Marek would take the little one's weight from her...

In a tiny bedroom in a cottage on Springhill Farm, Ruby Laird sat at the bedside of a sleeping child – the child she adored, the child she thought she would never have.

No bairn in Scotland would be better loved.

Tam, too, would lay down his life for this sweet blessing on their warm, contented marriage.

'I'll be here when your Ishbel wakes, Rowena,' she whispered. 'I'll always be here for her.

'She'll want for nothing. And when the time comes, she'll hae her share o' the farm that's aye been her home.

'Letting her go like this was the kindest thing you could have done – and I know it was the hardest. Visit us soon, Rowena.'

The light from a paraffin lamp made the crystal earrings lying on the table beside Ishbel's bed sparkle like precious jewels.

A mother's gift...

Ruby touched them tenderly but made no move to pick them up.

'Jewels for our jewel,' she whispered, smiling fondly.

The publishers hope that this book has given you enjoyable reading. Large Print Books are especially designed to be as easy to see and hold as possible. If you wish a complete list of our books please ask at your local library or write directly to:

Magna Large Print Books
Magna House, Long Preston,
Skipton, North Yorkshire.
BD23 4ND

This Large Print Book, for people
who cannot read normal print,
is published under the auspices of

THE ULVERSCROFT FOUNDATION

Other MAGNA Titles
In Large Print

LYN ANDREWS
Angels Of Mercy

HELEN CANNAM
Spy For Cromwell

EMMA DARCY
The Velvet Tiger

SUE DYSON
Fairfield Rose

J. M. GREGSON
To Kill A Wife

MEG HUTCHINSON
A Promise Given

TIM WILSON
A Singing Grave

RICHARD WOODMAN
The Cruise Of The Commissioner